"There's been a lot of trouble between me and J.R. over the years," Gary explained.

"What difference does it make? We're talking about a business loan here. Fifty thousand dollars!" Abby insisted.

The lines around Gary's mouth deepened. "You don't know my brother. It's not a simple loan—it's business. And doing business with J.R. . . ."

". . . will keep you out of a wheelchair. Get smart. It's the only way, and you'd better recognize that before it's too late!"

———————

Series Story Editor **Mary Ann Cooper** is America's foremost soap opera expert. She writes the nationally syndicated column *Speaking of Soaps*, is a major contributor to soap opera magazines, and has appeared on numerous radio and television talk shows.

Author **Marcia Lawrence** has lived most of her life in the Pacific Northwest. With two children, she splits her time between writing and making trips to soccer games, the dentist and birthday parties.

Dear Friend,

Our offices have been buzzing with excitement lately. Can you guess why? We're compiling material for our newest Soaps & Serials books.

Pioneer is proud to announce the addition of three outstanding shows to the Soaps & Serials line:

GENERAL HOSPITAL
ALL MY CHILDREN
ONE LIFE TO LIVE

We'll be introducing these new releases with a festive splash. Look for them! And don't miss our new and exciting features in forthcoming Soaps & Serials books.

For Soaps & Serials books,

Mary Ann Cooper

Mary Ann Cooper

P.S. If you've been searching for previous volumes of Soaps & Serials books and can't find them in your local book source, please see the order form inserted in this book.

KNOTS LANDING™

10

Family Affairs

From the television series created by David Jacobs

Soaps™
& Serials

PIONEER COMMUNICATIONS NETWORK, INC.

Family Affairs

From the television series KNOTS LANDING™
created by David Jacobs. This book is based on
scripts written by Robert W. Gilmer and David
Paulsen.

KNOTS LANDING™ paperback novels are
published and distributed by Pioneer
Communications Network, Inc.

ISBN: 0-916217-70-1

Printed in Canada

10 9 8 7 6 5 4 3 2 1

Family Affairs

Chapter One
Battle Lines

Gary Ewing was in trouble—big trouble—and there was just no way of getting out of it. He needed time and money, and he had neither.

From his office he saw the red Porsche as it wheeled into the parking lot of Knots Landing Motors. Slowly he got up from his desk and stared pensively through the window.

The Arizona license plates winked in the brilliant California sun, and the knot in his stomach tightened into a hard ball as the occupants of the car, two burly men wearing sunglasses and pin-striped suits, climbed out.

Recognizing Roy and Frank, Gary walked away from the window to the back door of his office and thought about his options. He could either face the two thugs from the Orchid Cab Company or he could run—if he could get away. And even if he could, what about Abby? She was as involved as he was.

Cursing the fact that he hadn't listened to

Sid, Gary opened the door and walked quickly down a long hallway used only by employees of the company. He thought about his dealings with the two men outside the building—about what a fool he'd been.

His first meeting with Frank Korshak and Roy Lance had brought him so much excitement and promise. The initial order of fifteen cars and the prospect of the cab company's large and rapid expansion in the Los Angeles area had clearly led Gary into a state of overexuberance.

Sid Fairgate, owner of Knots Landing Motors, had warned him countless times to slow down and "check those guys out." But the lure of big money, the desire to put together an impressive deal and a chance at really making a name for himself in Knots Landing had clouded Gary's judgment.

Even Sid's discovery that the Orchid Cab Company wasn't listed with the Better Business Bureau or recorded in any Albuquerque phone directory couldn't deter Gary from his headlong plunge toward destruction.

When Frank and Roy had come to Gary with a spare parts inventory contract, Sid had seen right through the scam and instinctively known that the deal was something to stay away from. The true value of the parts they had offered and their price tag of fifty thousand dollars had convinced Sid of only one thing: stolen goods. But Gary had chosen to look the other way.

"Sid, we're not running a Sunday school here," Gary had reasoned. "We're running a business!"

When Sid had held fast and refused to involve the company, Gary had entered into a verbal contract behind his boss's back.

Now he was paying for his rash decision—maybe with his life.

Beginning to sweat nervously, he slipped out the back door of the concrete building, hoping that the two men might not notice him as he sneaked through the repair shop.

He had no such luck.

Roy, the bigger of the two goons, grabbed him by the collar and pushed him hard, slamming him against the building. Gary fell backward and his head cracked against the concrete as he was pinned against the wall. The ringing in his ears and the distinctive taste of blood down the back of his throat made him realize even more the danger of dealing with the likes of the two thugs. All because of greed—his greed.

Frank leaned against the Porsche and slid a toothpick from one side of his mouth to the other.

Gary struggled but was thwarted by Roy's brute strength. He tried to kick his attacker, but Roy sidestepped the blow and slammed his shoulder against the wall. Pain seared through Gary's back and arm.

"Goin' somewhere?" Frank asked, a satisfied grin sliding across his face.

"Just around back."

"Sure."

"A deal's a deal," Roy said, his broad face so close that Gary could see the sweat trickling down his sideburns and the large pores bridging his nose.

"There's no way around that," Frank agreed.

"Look, I can't—" But another blow to his ribs knocked his breath away before he could finish the sentence. Dazed, he looked beyond his tormentors to the steady stream of traffic moving in front of the building. Maybe someone would see what Frank and Roy were doing.

And then what? he thought. *Will I be able to face Sid with the truth?*

Unfortunately, there was no escape.

Roy gave him another bone-jarring shove. "We already gave you a week. A bright boy like you—"

"I can't come up with fifty thousand dollars!"

"No? How about a few more days?"

"Days . . . months . . ." Gary was nearly frantic.

Roy turned to Frank with a hearty laugh. "This guy. He can get anything out of me. Okay. Today's Tuesday, right? We'll give you some more time. Thursday or maybe the weekend. Then again, maybe not." Releasing him, he patted Gary on the side of the face and continued, "But you're getting away with murder."

"Look, I won't have the money—"

But as Gary tried to explain, Roy straightened his cuffs and cut him off with a smug leer. Frank laughed, slid into the idling Porsche, and put the flashy car into gear. Roy squared his shoulders, walked over to the car and lowered himself into the passenger seat.

With a squeal of tires, the car roared out of

the parking lot, leaving Gary with a sick feeling of impending doom. *They enjoyed scaring the hell out of me,* he thought angrily as he stemmed the flow of blood from his mouth and then rubbed a bruise on his shoulder. *And they'll be back!*

Abby Cunningham sat frozen in front of her office intercom. Frank and Roy were threatening Gary, roughing him up! Her heart hammering with fear, she listened to the heated exchange and cringed when she heard the blows against his body. She thought about calling the police, but knew she couldn't. The police would only complicate things. More likely than not both she and Gary would be implicated in the stolen parts scheme.

She heard the Porsche roar out of the parking lot and was relieved to see Gary stagger back to his office. Resisting the urge to run to him, she slowly let out her breath. *Calm yourself, Abby. Use your head. You're into this up to your eyeballs and you know it!*

The two thugs from the Orchid Cab Company were serious about hurting Gary. Dead serious. Something had to be done to save his neck. But what?

Pushing back the desk chair, she ran her fingers nervously through her hair and began pacing between her desk and the window, trying to come up with a way to help Gary. He was more than just another co-worker or neighbor. She found him . . . attractive. Very attractive.

Today wasn't the first time she'd seen Gary dealing with Frank and Roy. Several weeks earlier Gary had met with the men and proved himself to be willing to take a few risks for the sake of ambition.

His ambition was what had first attracted her to him. She liked the sense of ruthlessness and power that came with ambition. The fact that Gary was tall and good looking—with straw-blond hair and brilliant blue eyes—didn't hurt, either. And, of course, there was the money. Gary was tied to big money: Ewing Oil money. No doubt about it, Gary Ewing was everything she wanted in a man.

And now he was in danger of losing his life!

Unless she could come up with a plan. She continued to pace the office, glancing occasionally to the door and wondering if she should go to Gary and console him. In frustration she picked up the morning newspaper from the corner of her desk and wadded it into a ball before stopping short and smiling to herself.

Pushing aside the ledgers and invoices for the company she spread the business section of the paper on her desk and smoothed it out. There, on the second page, was a picture of the one man who would be able to help: Gary's brother, J.R. Ewing.

What a godsend! J.R. in Knots Landing; nothing could be more perfect. She sat on the corner of her desk and ignored the work piled around her. As her plan jelled, Abby smiled and reached for the phone.

A few hours later, Abby was still congratulating herself on her phone call to J.R. Hearing his soft Texan drawl and the power in his voice had been exhilarating. She'd rewarded herself by leaving the office a little early and sunbathing on her chaise longue by the pool in her back yard.

Dozing fitfully, she heard Richard before she saw him. "Thought I saw you sneak in early," he said as he ducked his head through the back yard gate. Smiling, he lifted a bottle of vodka into the air. "I took the afternoon off. Thought we could celebrate together."

"Celebrate? Celebrate what?"

He walked toward her and placed the bottle on the portable bar. "Anything you want."

"Sounds good to me," she said, rolling to her side and watching as he mixed them drinks. She was in such a good mood she wasn't even going to be mad at Richard for coming over unannounced.

"You should call, you know. The kids could have been home."

"But I already know they're with Jeff." He handed her a drink and clinked his glass with hers. "To us."

She smiled and sipped her drink, her thoughts still on J.R. Richard set his drink on a table; then, pulling off his shirt, he dove into the pool. He swam the length under water, grabbed a quick breath at the opposite end, and then swam back. Shaking the water from his hair, he hoisted himself over the edge and returned to the chair next to hers.

"What was that all about?"

He grinned and put on his sunglasses. "Just showing off."

"That's what I thought." She finished her drink and rolled over.

Richard stretched his bare legs in front of him and slowly sipped his drink, enjoying the warm feel in the pit of his stomach as the screwdriver took hold.

Abby ignored him. Her mind was on a million different things—all of them involving J.R. Ewing and his money.

She'd hoped to relax and take a short nap by the pool before she was forced to return to reality and the fact that Jeff was bringing the kids home soon. But Richard changed all that. With a sigh, she closed her eyes.

The sun danced off her blond curls and she shifted to her back to allow the warm rays full access to her already tan body. Tugging at the skimpy electric-blue fabric of her bikini, she smiled to herself as she imagined her meeting with J.R.

Her movement caught Richard's attention. Grinning lazily, he walked over to the chaise, bent down, and kissed her lightly on the lips.

She stirred slightly, but motioned for him to leave her alone. She wanted to think. "Richard—" Abby was interrupted by another kiss. "Richard, don't!" Reluctantly opening her eyes, she sat up and forcefully pushed him away from her.

He sat back down on his chair and pouted. "I thought you were going to sleep all day."

"So did I!" Good Lord, he could be such a pain! Accepting the fact that he wasn't going to leave her alone, she got up, stretched, and walked across the hot cement to the portable bar. Squinting against the late afternoon sun, she poured herself a tall glass of juice. She lifted her hair from her neck and placed the cool glass against her cheek.

Richard found her every move provocative. He watched her return to the chaise and stared pointedly at the juice glass. "Orange juice . . . and no vodka?"

"No more. Not today." She yawned and stretched again. "What time is it?"

He glanced at his watch and moved closer to her. "Quarter to five. When's Jeff bringing the kids back?"

"Probably around six."

"That gives us another hour . . ." Leaning over, Richard tried to nuzzle Abby's neck but she slid out of reach.

". . . of sun," she finished, and then feeling a little contrite for snapping at him, added, "Would you put some oil on my back?"

"I thought you'd never ask." He set his drink near the pool and grabbed the suntan oil off the table as she rolled onto her stomach. His oiled fingers slid sensuously over her bare skin and she made a sound of pleasure. Smiling to himself, Richard attempted to move the swim suit's straps so that he could touch more of her supple skin . . .

She took hold of his arm to stop him. "Richard . . ."

"You'll get lines."

Abby sighed and removed her hand.

Sensing she was about to give in, he moved the string and began massaging the skin over her shoulders in circular motions. She sighed and Richard's oiled fingers slid lower, to the small of her back. Abby's skin glistened in the late afternoon sunlight. A soft breeze rustled through the palm trees near the house and lifted a few sweat-dampened curls from her cheek.

Richard was weak with his need for her. "Turn over and I'll do the front," he suggested.

"The back's good enough," she said, suddenly irritated again and wondering why she put up with him. Unhappy in his marriage to Laura, Richard was becoming a pest. Besides, she had other fish to fry. She smothered a grin as she thought about her upcoming meeting with J.R. Ewing. Now there was a real man!

Jeff Cunningham was worried. As he drove away from the burger shack near the ocean, he couldn't think about anything but his family— or what was left of his family. After spending a day with his children at the beach, he was appalled at their manners and attitudes: typically laid-back, Southern California, apathetic "anything goes."

What kind of mother was Abby? Sometimes he wondered if she gave a damn about the kids.

As he drove Olivia and Brian home, he watched them eating hot dogs, burgers, fries, and milk shakes. Olivia was sitting next to him in the front seat, stuffing another french fry into her mouth and staring out the window at the white sand of the beach. Teenagers were playing volleyball, sun worshipers were glistening with oil, and surfers were still waist-deep in the clear blue sea, hoping to catch the next big wave. But Jeff didn't notice. He was too wrapped up in his own problems.

Shaking his head, he turned to his daughter and indicated the remains of her dinner. "You know what that junk does to you?"

"Mr. Avery says it grows hair on your chest," Brian said.

"I'm getting a little tired of hearing that name." Jeff's fingers tightened around the steering wheel. With one eye on the road ahead, he looked into the rear-view mirror and saw Brian take another big bite of his hot dog, smearing mustard over his chin.

Olivia slid lower in the front seat. "How do you think we feel? You only have to *hear* about him."

"So how come he's around so much?"

Brian shrugged and rolled his eyes. "He comes over to make goo-goo eyes over Mom!"

"Great . . . just great." Jeff muttered, his brows drawing down over his eyes. What was the matter with Abby? Why was she carrying on with the neighbor? Sometimes he wondered if his ex-wife ever used that beautiful head of hers! Scowling, he followed the road inland and considered the best and worst years of his life—the years when he'd been married to Abby.

Damn her. Why had it all gone wrong?

When they'd first met, Abby had overwhelmed him with her charm, intelligence, sophistication and beauty. He'd been drawn to her like a magnet. Time with Abby had seemed to fly by and had left him longing for their next encounter. She always had a knack for making

him feel proud and happy. And physically—
well, one look and Jeff was still under her spell.
Even after all of the anger and pain.

Olivia tapped him on the shoulder, bringing
him abruptly back to the present. Brian was
looking out the window with a puzzled expression. "Hey, Dad! Where are we going?"

"What?"

The kids started laughing and bouncing in
their seats. "You just drove by our street!"

Disgusted with himself, Jeff slammed on the
brakes, put the car into reverse and backed up
to turn into the cul-de-sac. He kept telling himself that this particular street was a good place
for the kids to grow up. Well-kept houses,
friendly neighbors, not too far from the beach.
So why did the uncomfortable knot in his stomach tighten every time he brought the kids
back?

Abby heard a door slam and the sound of
excited voices. Lifting her head, she saw Olivia
and Brian burst through the door and run into
the back yard.

Olivia was carrying a cage with a little rabbit
in it, and Brian was lugging a huge stuffed dog.

"Mommy, Mommy, look what Daddy brought
me!" Olivia said.

Scarcely able to contain himself, Brian broke
in, "Look what he bought me!"

Abby sat up on the chaise, struggling to keep
the front of her suit in place. Damn Jeff and his
miserable timing; he wasn't supposed to bring
the kids home for at least another hour!

Richard didn't move. He remained leaning

over Abby with oil still dripping from his fingers. He attempted to look interested in the kids' new treasures, but he failed miserably.

In their excitement, both children spoke at once about the new additions to the household. Olivia peered happily into the rabbit's cage. "Her name is Rita."

Brian, holding up his wiry-haired stuffed animal for all to see, proudly informed Abby, "It's nearly two feet tall!"

With a tender smile Olivia wiggled a finger in the rabbit's cage and said, "She's going to live in my room."

"Hold it." Abby's eyes rolled toward the sky as she silently cursed Jeff and searched for the right words to put a gentle yet effective end to the game plan. *Rabbits and more toys! Why is Jeff always trying to buy the kids' love?*

Jeff pushed open the gate and walked into the back yard. He glanced at Richard Avery leaning over his ex-wife. Though he felt an unwanted surge of jealousy, Jeff tried to ignore the feeling as he followed the stone path that cut across the grass and led to the pool.

"Mom, my stomach hurts," Brian complained. He made a face, dropped his toy on the patio and abruptly sat down next to his mother.

Draping an arm around her son, Abby looked down at him. "You are a little pale," she said as she placed her hand on his forehead. "Oh, honey . . . I hope it's not the flu."

"It's a chili dog, chocolate shake, and fries if you want to know," Jeff explained, disgusted that he'd given in to the kids' demands.

"*Large* fries," corrected Olivia.

Turning to Jeff, Abby didn't bother to hide her own irritation. "I thought you hated giving them junk food."

"That's all they'll eat. It's what they're used to."

Shooting a killing glance at Jeff, Abby turned her attention to her son. "Bring me the white bottle from the medicine cabinet, sweetie."

Brian nodded and then, still holding his stomach, hurried off toward the house. Olivia gathered up her things and, whispering explanations to her new pet, followed her brother inside.

An awkward moment of silence ensued. Feeling like an intruder, Richard stood and coughed quietly to get Abby's attention.

She caught the hint and forced a grin. "Well, I guess it's time for the perfunctory introductions. Jeff Cunningham . . . Richard Avery. And vice versa."

Stepping forward, Richard extended his hand. "I'm one of the neighbors. I live next door."

"I'm the ex-husband. I used to live in." Jeff reached for Richard's hand and noticed it was covered with oil. His eyes narrowed and his lips twisted downward. "Looks like you've had your hands full."

Before Richard could respond, Brian ran across the yard proudly holding up a bottle for his mother's inspection.

Abby laughed and shook her head before waving him back inside the house. "That's the shoe polish. Go back in and bring the little white bottle."

Slapping his forehead in mock disgust, Brian

turned back to the house.

Jeff's simmering irritation exploded into anger at Abby. "Shoe polish in the medicine cabinet? What if he drank some of it?"

"Why would he drink shoe polish?"

"If he thought it were medicine—"

"I'd have to tie him down to get him to take it."

"Abby, he's only seven years old!"

"Spare me."

Furious, Jeff rubbed his hand over his jaw, thinking about telling Abby and her miserable friend off. Then, realizing that chastising her wouldn't do a bit of good, he strode across the yard to the patio.

"Leaving so soon?" Abby asked hopefully.

"Don't hold your breath."

"What do you mean?"

"Just that I'm not leaving until I've checked the house."

"Checked the house? Now, wait a minute."

But it was too late. Jeff had already disappeared into the kitchen, determined to perform a safety check of the house.

Muttering to herself about his self-righteous, "holier-than-thou" attitude, Abby got off the chaise, threw on a cover-up and, cursing her luck, hurried inside to get rid of him. She had too much to think about to worry about shoe polish, medicine, and whatever else Jeff decided to panic over.

Richard started to follow her inside, then thought better of it. Instead, he grabbed a beach towel from the chaise to wipe the oil from his hands.

Steaming, Abby entered the kitchen to find
Jeff going through the cabinet under the sink.
"What do you think you're doing?"

He ignored her.

"Jeff!"

He yanked items out to read their labels, then
started tossing bottles and boxes into the middle of the white and tan linoleum floor. "Window cleaner, scouring pads, dish-washing
liquid . . . look at all this stuff."

"This is ridiculous!" She crossed her arms
over her chest and tried to ignore the mess in
the middle of the floor. "Besides, the dangerous things—bleach, oven cleaner, disinfectant—
are all kept over the stove." She pointed over
his head to the highest cabinet. "There. See?
I can barely reach them."

Jeff stopped and silently counted to ten.
When he looked up at her, his mouth was set
in a harsh line but his eyes took all of her in.
Slim, tan, a figure that wouldn't quit, and lumi-
nous blue-green eyes. Abby was still the most
gorgeous woman he'd ever met. And he
wanted her. Damn it, he wanted her. Right
here, right now, right in the middle of the
kitchen floor with her lover just outside the
door!

Knowing he was still her fool, and angry with
himself as much as with her, he glared at the
scattered bottles and boxes on the floor, trying
to come up with some other excuse to continue
the argument. "You know, that junk food you
feed them is almost as bad as this poison!"

"*You* bought them lunch," she reminded
him.

"Brian won't eat anything else, thanks to you and your 'friend.'"

"What's Richard got to do with this?"

Yes, what? Richard thought as he walked through the door and leaned against the wall. He positioned himself close to Abby and touched her possessively on the shoulder.

Abby jerked away from Richard. She was still seething, but she didn't want an out-and-out battle with Jeff. Not yet, anyway. Too much was at stake.

His jaw clenched tightly, Jeff walked to the other side of the room. He shoved his hands into his pockets and tried to lean against the counter, but the tension in his muscles kept his body taut to the point that his muscles ached. He hated thinking about any other man with Abby or his children, and this sleaze of a "neighbor" was no exception. Just the thought of Avery slathering her with suntan oil, kissing her, letting his hands run all over her body. . . .

He couldn't stand the torment a minute longer. With the thought of them making love pounding in his head, Jeff brushed past Abby as he strode toward the hallway and the front of the house.

"You going to say good-bye to the kids?" Abby called after him.

"I already did," Jeff tossed back as he walked into the bright afternoon sunlight and slammed the door so hard it rattled the window panes.

Chapter Two
Betrayals

Jeff stood motionless in the driveway of Abby's home. A million angry thoughts raced through his mind. The reverie was broken when he focused on the Fairgate house next door. Before the divorce, Sid and Karen had been a part of his family; now they were just friends.

He started up their drive slowly and deliberately, as if trying to convince himself that bringing Sid and Karen into the fight was the right thing to do.

Hesitating for just a moment, he knocked on the front door and stood in a stiff pose with hands jammed down into his pant pockets. He looked as miserable as he felt.

Within a couple of seconds the door opened.

''Jeff!'' Karen Fairgate's surprise gave way to happiness, and she threw her arms around him. Stepping back for a better look, she teased, ''You look terrible.''

''Thanks. Just what I need to hear.''

"Trouble?" She looked past him to Abby's house. Unfortunately, with Abby there was always trouble.

"Have you got a minute?"

"For you?". Karen grabbed his arm and led him into the house. "Always. Come on, I'll buy you a cup of coffee."

Once in the kitchen, she motioned for him to take a seat at the table. Jeff dropped into one of the cane-backed chairs near the window and stared through the glass and across the street.

"Okay, out with it. What's going on?" Karen asked, pouring two mugs of coffee and setting one in front of him.

Brooding, he silently noted the cut flowers on the table, the homey atmosphere of the house.

"I wish I knew."

"Well, it must be something for you to come storming over here looking as if you were ready to kill."

Jeff frowned into his cup. "You sure you want to know?"

"Shoot." She took a chair near the table and sipped her coffee as Jeff pinched his eyes shut and leaned back. Reluctantly, he told her about the blow-up with Abby.

"I don't know," Jeff said. "Maybe I'm over-reacting. What do you think?"

"Well, it's natural for you to be concerned about the kids."

"Then you agree—I'm not overreacting. That stuff's too dangerous to leave under a sink where the kids can get at it."

"What kind of stuff?" Sid asked as he entered the room and greeted Jeff with a friendly pat on the shoulder.

"You name it. Window cleaner, ammonia, lye!"

Sid arched a brow as he poured himself a cup of coffee. "Lye? What on earth would Abby be doing with lye?"

"Well, it was the drain opener stuff—that's got lye in it. And it's all just sitting there, like a bomb waiting to explode. I don't know. Maybe I make too much of everything." Jeff paused. "Maybe I should just say, 'Abby, you really shouldn't leave stuff like this around,' instead of flying off the handle the way I do."

Karen touched him gently on the hand. "No one ever accused you and Abby of bringing out the best in each other."

Jeff laughed cynically. "That's certainly true."

Sid took a swallow of coffee and grimaced. "Can I get you a *real* drink?"

"Please. Scotch. Anything. But let me ask you something, Karen." The lines on his forehead deepened. "Abby and that Avery fellow— is he it, or is there a steady stream of guys coming and going?"

"Oh, no, Jeff, don't be silly!"

Jeff felt a wave of relief wash over him.

Karen finished her coffee. "Just Richard, as far as I know."

"Karen!" Sid snapped. But it was too late.

Jeff felt as if he'd just been kicked in the stomach. So it was true. Even though he'd suspected Abby of having an affair, the news was a blow to his ego. Renewed anger tightened his jaw and it was all he could do not to smash his fist against the wall.

Disgusted with herself, Karen realized that she had been trapped into an admission. She got up from the table and placed her cup on the counter. "Look, Jeff, I'm not even sure about Richard."

"Well, I'm sure! The kids as much as told me. It's amazing how much they pick up. Dammit all, anyway." He clenched his fist and stood. Walking across the kitchen, he glared through the window at Abby's house. Was Richard Avery such a bastard that he would continue to hang around Abby even though the kids were home? Jeff smiled to himself when he thought about the oil on Richard's hands and the fact that by arriving home early, he'd managed to break up their afternoon tryst.

Sid had slipped into the family room and poured Jeff three fingers of scotch. When he returned to the kitchen, Jeff was still staring through the window. "Here."

Jeff took the drink and tossed it back in one swallow. It burned his throat and fed his need for revenge.

"Jeff, you're working yourself up for nothing. Richard was out of work, hanging around. You know Abby. She took advantage of his availability. But now he's got a new job . . . out of the picture." Sid tried to explain while glancing at Karen and silently warning her not to blow it again.

Karen caught the hint and held her tongue.

"I think I better start keeping closer track of the kids . . . come by a little more often," Jeff said.

Sid ran his fingers through his dark hair. "If Abby feels spied on . . ."

"I'm not talking about spying."

"Yes, you are," Karen said, ignoring Sid's glance. "You're talking about spying."

"You're right. I am. What is it with me?"

Karen gave him a sympathetic smile. "You're human, like the rest of us. It's incurable."

"I know, I know. But we've been separated a year and in some ways, nothing has changed. I used to hate going to bed angry with Abby. I'd get this awful feeling in my stomach and I'd have to make up with her. I've got that same feeling now."

"Abby's still home," Sid suggested.

Some of his anger melted away. "I guess it'd be a shame if Abby and I turned into one of those awful divorced couples whose sole aim in life was to make each other miserable," he said, staring at the empty glass. "Thanks for the drink and the good advice."

After shaking Sid's hand and promising Karen that he wouldn't be such a stranger, Jeff started to leave.

Boiling inside, Sid walked him to the front door. Once Jeff was gone, he marched straight back into the kitchen. What right did Karen have sticking her nose into Abby's life? "Karen?"

She held her hands up in surrender. "I know, I know. I got trapped."

"*He* trapped you."

"Come on, Sid," Karen said sadly. "He's not that clever. Manipulation is Abby's game, not Jeff's."

Still glaring at her, Sid finished his scotch and tried to remain calm. It was impossible—but then again, it always was when Abby was involved. "I wish we had instant replay. You'd see how he manipulated you."

"Lighten up, will you? Anyway, I'm not sure that Jeff's worried for nothing."

"Abby's kids are fine! She just has a different philosophy of parenting than you, that's all." Still angry, he sat down at the kitchen table and dropped his hands into his head.

"Right. 'Less is more.'" Karen said gently and kissed the top of his head.

Shaking his head, he hoped to God that he was right and that everything would turn out okay. With Abby, the future was hard to predict.

Abby held the long black sheath in front of her and eyed her reflection in the mirror. "Too morbid," she told herself and threw the dress on the bed with two others. She dug into the closet again and pulled out a silk dress with a long slit. The blue was the same shade as her eyes.

Smiling, she held the dress to her neck and tilted her head. *Yep, this is the dress guaranteed to knock any man's socks off, J.R. Ewing included.*

Her spirits had risen once she'd managed to get rid of Richard and could concentrate on her visit to J.R.'s hotel room.

She lifted her blond curls off her neck and smiled at the sophisticated woman in the mirror. "Mr. Ewing, watch out," she whispered with a laugh before she looked out the window and saw Jeff heading her way. His compressed lips, his bunched shoulders, his tight jaw and the storm brewing in his eyes suggested that he was ready for another fight.

"Wonderful," she murmured, tossing the blue dress onto the pile on the bed and heading downstairs. "Just what I need!"

As Jeff walked the short distance between the two houses, he recalled his life with Abby in the "good ol' days." It seemed like years since he'd watched the kids ride their tricycles and bicycles around the neighborhood. He missed the kids and the barbecues on warm summer evenings. He missed the laughter, the fun, the anticipation of each new day. And he missed Abby. Loath as he was to admit it, he missed her so badly he ached late at night alone in his bed.

Telling himself he was a fool, Jeff hesitated a moment at Abby's front door and then lifted the heavy brass knocker.

When Abby opened the door, he was struck again by her beauty. Wide sea-blue eyes looked up at him suspiciously, and he felt instant regret.

He gestured expansively. "Look, I'm sorry about what happened earlier."

Abby stepped onto the front porch and shrugged knowingly. "A long weekend . . . the kids . . . I understand, believe me." When she smiled, her entire face softened.

Encouraged, he grinned. "Hey, how about dinner? Just you and me."

She hesitated. "I . . . I don't think so. I want the kids in bed early. Besides, I haven't seen them for several days. I missed them."

"Lunch, then? In a couple of days?"

"I don't know—"

"We need to talk."

"About what?"

So she insisted on baiting him. He sighed and tried not to get angry. It was damned near impossible. When he was with Abby, the sparks always flew. "You know I'm concerned about the kids."

"Jeff, the kids are fine. I wish you would stop worrying about them."

"I just don't think that they should be exposed to certain things."

"We've been all through that. There's no way they can get to anything that will harm them. Besides, they're good kids; they never get into that kind of trouble."

His anger starting to get the better of him, he snapped, "I'm not talking about the cleaning supplies."

"Well, what then?"

"I don't like your affair with Richard being thrown in their faces!"

Stunned, Abby didn't move, but just stared at him. *"What!"*

Jeff's eyes narrowed and he crossed his arms over his chest. "I know that you are having an affair with Avery."

Abby looked over Jeff's shoulder. Fortunately there was no one outside to overhear the exchange. "That's none of your business. And even if it were, what makes you think so?"

"Oh, come on, Abby. I'm not blind, and people do talk."

"Nobody could talk about something they don't know about. You're just fishing and I hate it. I always have!"

"Don't give me your phony indignation, Abby," Jeff said, his lips twisting into a hateful grin. "Karen as much as confirmed it."

She tried to walk back into the house and slam the door in his face, but he grabbed her arm. Abby glanced down at the hand restraining her. Indignant rage sparked in her eyes. "I want you out of here right now. And stay out!" She glanced across the street as she pulled her arm free. *Just wait till I get a hold of that busybody.*

"This isn't over, Abby," he warned. "I'm not going to let you do this to my kids."

"They're my kids, too. Don't you ever forget that, *and* who has custody."

"I remember. But maybe things will change," Jeff shouted as he spun around and stalked out of the house.

Abby slammed the door and paced around the room, seething. How dare Karen give Jeff that information? What did Jeff mean, "this isn't over" and "maybe things will change?" Why was her life getting so complicated? she wondered. Why now?

Valene was in the kitchen putting the finishing touches on dinner when she heard Gary come through the front door and hurry into the bedroom.

How odd, she thought, missing the usual kiss he gave her when he came home. Seeing that the stew was simmering just as it should, she put the lid back on the kettle and walked through the house to the bedroom. The door was closed. She pushed it open.

Gary was changing his clothes. He'd put on a pair of jeans and was slipping a shirt over his head. His movements were quick, but not quick enough. Valene gasped when she saw the red and blue welt on his shoulder.

"What happened to you?" she asked.

He turned around and offered her a sheepish grin. "Nothin' much. Just wasn't lookin' when some inventory in the parts department came through."

Valene walked over to him and touched the bruise. Gary winced and pulled his shirt over his head.

"I don't understand," she said, her brows drawn over her eyes in worry.

"If you want to know the truth—"

"I do."

Gary avoided her eyes and tucked his shirt into his pants. "One of the guys was pushing a load of transmission housings through the service department. He ran into me. It was an accident." He looked at her and smiled. "I'll recover."

"You're sure?" she asked, unconvinced but hoping that Gary was telling her the truth.

"Sure, I'm sure."

"Then I don't have to worry about you being in some sort of trouble?"

Inwardly groaning, Gary forced a grin. "Of course not." He kissed her on the cheek. "Now, how about dinner? I'm starved."

"It's just about ready," she replied, lost in thought. She couldn't shake the feeling that Gary was hiding something from her. Something dangerous.

* * *

Karen opened the front door and just barely got out of the way as the full wrath and fury of Abby went blowing past her into the living room.

"How dare you tell Jeff I was having an affair!" Abby accused, her cheeks flushed.

"I—I didn't," Karen said, stammering.

"Yes, you did. I know when he's lying and he isn't. You told him I was having an affair with Richard."

Cornered, Karen tried to explain. "Look, it wasn't like that. If anything, I was defending you."

"Then get off of my side." Abby sat down on the sofa, crossed her legs and tried to count to ten.

"Listen, Abby . . . calm down. Jeff came in here acting as if he knew about you and Richard . . . and implying that you've had an army of lovers."

"Terrific. So you said, not an army, just Richard."

"Not exactly. I . . ." Karen shrugged and lifted her palms in defeat. "Well, something like that."

"Great!" Seething, Abby shook her head. "He's amazing. Really amazing. And if you don't mind my asking, where did you come off saying anything? Do you know for sure that Richard and I have been having an affair?"

"Come on, Abby—"

"I asked if you knew for sure." Abby's angry glare pinned her sister-in-law.

"I couldn't prove it, but—"

"Thank you. Want to know?"

"It won't make my day."

Looking Karen right in the eye, Abby raised one of her perfect eyebrows. "Well, the answer is yes. Richard and I have been to bed together. Isn't that deplorable?"

"Yes."

"Of course. Deplorable that a very nervous, very troubled man has something—one thing—in his life that makes him feel good. A pitiful marriage. A wife who's so full of herself that she has no room for him. All he has is wicked Abby, who makes him a little bit happy once in a while."

Karen couldn't believe her ears. Abby was trying to paint herself as some kind of martyred saint while she was sleeping with a married man. Karen couldn't hide the sarcasm in her voice. "How charitable of you. But can you deduct it from your income tax?"

"If there's a way, I'll find it."

Karen nearly laughed.

Turning on her heel, Abby tossed one last warning over her shoulder. "Stay out of my life and keep away from Jeff. Don't tell him anything else . . . I play dirty."

"Is that a threat?"

"No. A promise."

Kenny Ward sat on the edge of Sylvie's bed, leafing through various paste-ups for an album cover. The production work on Sylvie's next record had reached the stage of final approval of art work, and the perfect cover was critical.

Eyeing the different shots, he called over his

shoulder, ''Hey, Sylvie, what do you think of this picture for your new cover?''

Sylvie almost didn't hear him. She was leaning against the wall in the next room. She'd let Kenny's jacket slide from her hand to the floor and her fingers were clenched around the crisp, documented lie.

''Honey?'' Kenny repeated.

Swallowing hard, Sylvie straightened her shoulders and marched into the bedroom, throwing the damning piece of evidence in Kenny's face.

To add insult to injury, Kenny didn't notice either the paper or her wrath. Instead, he continued looking at the paste-ups. ''This is good. Very good,'' he said almost to himself. ''It's a change of pace for you, but I think that it has a real good feeling.''

''How long have you known?'' she demanded, tears threatening her eyes.

''Known what?'' He looked up, saw her ramrod stiff body, the anger in her eyes, her thin, rigid, jean-clad legs and her arms crossed firmly over her chest. Glancing at the paper that had fluttered to the floor, Kenny recognized the divorce papers that Ginger had recently served him. He thought a minute and then realized that the jig was up.

''Where did you find this?'' he demanded, scooping the legal document from the floor and trying to take the offensive.

''I needed some money and I went through your jacket pockets.''

Overplaying his rage, Kenny crumpled the already-wrinkled paper and stuffed it into the pocket of his jeans. "I don't want you going through my things."

"Of course you don't—it makes it harder for you to lie to me when I do."

"I didn't lie to you."

"Your wife's divorcing you! And you never told me. That's not lying, buddy boy?"

A muscle twitched in his jaw. "I guess I wasn't ready to talk about it yet."

"How dare you keep a secret like that from me?" Sylvie flung herself onto the bed.

"Sylvie, I don't have to tell you everything that goes on in my life."

"We're talking about my life, too!"

"Your life?" Kenny repeated, finally understanding some of her fury. "Wait a minute. Were you thinking of marrying me?"

Sylvie bit back an automatic yes. "No . . ."

Kenny got off the bed and leaned against the window sill. "Hey, remember, we've got no strings, no ties to each other, you know that."

"I know . . . but if you're divorced, we could look for a place together. Really live together, instead of you just staying here." After pausing for a breath and softening her tone she continued, "We could start all over again. Just you and me, without the shadow of your wife hanging over us."

Kenny looked at her, long and hard. She looked so small and vulnerable huddled on the corner of the bed. "It's not going to work," he said gently.

"Why not? We're good together, Kenny—"

"But, it's never enough, Sylvie. You're always asking for more. It's just not going to work."

Sylvie slumped backward against the wall and visibly paled. Her mind scrambled for the right combination of words. "How could I love you too much? I thought that's what you wanted?"

"I want to produce good records," he said. He looked away from her guiltily. "And, I want my wife back. That's what I want."

"But, Kenny—"

"If you still want to work with me, fine. If not, it's the chance I have to take. But if I don't end it with you, I'll never get Ginger back. That's a chance I won't take."

Kenny turned and strode purposefully out of the room. Sylvie was left standing speechless, with tears puddling in the corners of her eyes, her world suddenly thrown into painful turmoil.

Blowing a strand of blond hair out of her eyes, Laura Avery walked into her office, tossed her briefcase on a chair and sat down behind her large, walnut desk.

She was surprised to see a bouquet of flowers sitting on the corner of the desk.

Yellow roses? From Richard? She pushed aside the tissue paper and, blushing, opened the small card. Her heart nearly stopped. The card was simple. It said only "Thanks", but it was signed by one of Laura's clients, David Souther. Her blush deepened and she set the flowers aside.

Looking across the room at the abstract painting she'd purchased with her first commission check, Laura tried to collect her thoughts. The painting had been expensive, but she hadn't cared and there hadn't been a day since then that she hadn't stared at the bold blue and gray colors and experienced an inner tranquillity—something she desperately needed right now.

Absently she pinned her hair away from her face and thought about how complicated her life had become—complicated beyond her wildest dreams. For years she'd depended upon her husband, Richard, for support, both financial and psychological.

Suddenly, their safe little world had been blown wide open. He'd lost his job—or rather, quit it for another opportunity that had never crystallized. The blow to his ego had been devastating and he'd become sullen and defensive, to the point that their marriage was on shaky ground. And though he'd eventually found a position with another firm, things just weren't the same.

She glanced again at the flowers. Just then there was a soft tap at the door. An associate realtor, Scooter Warren, walked briskly into the room. Behind him was David.

"Come in, come in," Laura said, smiling despite her worries.

"Well, you finally got him, Laura," Scooter announced.

"Three months and five hundred open houses later," she added.

Slightly embarrassed, David tugged at his silk tie and pushed up the sleeves of his Brooks Brothers suit. "Hope I was worth it."

"You will be when you've finished signing these papers," Laura said, laughing as she handed David the escrow agreements and closing papers.

He signed the papers with a flourish, and Laura felt the exhilaration of a job well done when he handed them back to her.

Scooter rubbed his hands together and grinned from ear to ear. "Okay, we're finished. Who's for a celebration dinner?"

Laura was the first to decline. "Tonight? I can't."

"Tomorrow night?" Scooter suggested.

It was David's turn to delay the plans. "Can't make it. I teach school tomorrow night."

"Come on, you guys, loosen up. What about the next night? That's going to be my final offer," Scooter said with feigned irritation.

"Fine with me," David said.

"Okay, okay . . . the evening after tomorrow night, it is," Laura agreed.

The intercom buzzed, announcing a call for Scooter. "Hate to run out on you, but I hear money calling," he said as he left Laura's office.

David looked into Laura's eyes, hesitating for just a second. "Thanks for your patience. This house is going to be perfect for me."

"I've always known that. *You* were the one who had to be convinced."

"And I am. *You* convinced me."

Laura nodded. "I know." Staring into David's serious eyes made her heart race slightly and brought just a hint of a blush to her cheeks. "Thank you for the flowers."

"Thank you for helping me."

Slightly flustered, she walked around the

desk. "So . . . I'll see you for dinner in a couple of days?"

"I can't wait," David said softly.

Laura's heart nearly skipped a beat.

As he left the office, her eyes followed the outline of his body and she was forced to admit to herself that he was an extremely attractive man. Tall and lean, with a generous smile, he had the self-assurance and confidence that would make any woman look twice. Getting to know him better was tempting, to say the least.

As Laura sat at her desk in silent reflection, she stared at the vase of yellow roses and smiled sadly.

"David's a thoughtful guy, isn't he?" Scooter had returned and was following her gaze.

She hadn't even heard him enter. Slightly embarrassed, she nodded. "You're pretty smart, aren't you?"

Scooter shrugged and turned his palms to the ceiling. "Hey, I've got eyes. That's all."

"Think I should head him off at the pass?"

Scooter smiled and shook his head. "Don't ask me questions I can't answer, Laura," he said. Waving, he walked out of the room.

"Oh, Lord," Laura whispered. "What am I getting myself into?"

Chapter Three

Brotherly Love

J.R. Ewing

His name had a definite ring to it, he thought proudly. In Dallas it struck fear, commanded respect, evoked passion and love, stirred hatred, and demanded attention. People there still said that there was nothing worth seeing, hearing or doing that J.R. didn't already know about. Could his effect on Knots Landing be any different? J.R. wondered. Probably not.

He poured himself a drink and walked to the window of his hotel suite. Swirling the bourbon in his glass he stared over the rooftops of the city and out to the ocean. Calm and blue and serene, it still reminded him of the fiasco with Petrolux not more than a year ago. If he'd had his way, there would be oil rigs out on the ocean, pumping Ewing oil by the tankerful. Instead, his brother Gary had managed to rally to the town's environmental defense and force J.R. and Petrolux to an alternate, more costly

location. Though J.R. had managed to look like
a hero by moving the drilling location, it still
burned him that Gary had finally found the
nerve to stand up to him instead of drowning
himself in a bottle.

Still sipping his drink, he walked over to the
soft leather couch and sat down. The room had
style—thick carpet, expensive contemporary fur-
niture, tasteful paintings, and windows with a
view of the ocean. J.R. propped his snakeskin
boots up on the coffee table and waited, chuck-
ling to himself over the local news coverage of
his arrival. The oil industry trade show and
convention was a good reason to come and
check up on his interests in Los Angeles. But
little did the folks back at Southfork know all
the reasons for his trip to Knots Landing.

He glanced at his watch. He'd received a
phone call from a woman who had claimed she
needed to speak to him about his brother. The
desperation in her voice had worked; he'd
agreed to see her. J.R. had had a difficult time
assessing the woman's desires and motivations,
but she had succeeded in piquing his curiosity.
Besides, he wanted to check up on old Gary
and possibly find a way to get back at him.

If nothing else, J.R. knew he'd enjoy meeting
a mysterious woman who had the ability to
scheme and plan behind people's backs—fine
qualities in a woman, as long as he kept the
upper hand. And he would. No doubt about it.

J.R. smiled as he finished his drink.

In the lobby of the hotel, Abby stopped by a mirror to check her makeup and hair. She tugged at a

few blond tendrils, letting them escape wildly from the twist at her crown. The blue silk dress was perfect—sophisticated, but molding to her body and shimmering provocatively. Smiling, she recognized the effect she would most likely have on her new acquaintance.

She was already ten minutes late, so he would be waiting for her. Taking the elevator to the top floor, she hesitated for a moment at the door of the penthouse. Then, working up her courage, she knocked.

It was opened quickly.

He was all she expected and more. Tall, attractive, impeccably dressed. He offered her a pleasant, friendly smile.

"Well, I'll be damned," he said, his blue eyes assessing her as he beckoned her inside. "From the desperate tone in your voice on the phone I sure didn't expect a face like this."

Abby slid gracefully into the room and felt at ease with J.R. almost immediately. The man represented power and money, and Abby could almost hear his mind working.

"Can I get you a drink?"

"White wine, if you have it."

"A lady's drink," he said, his eyes bright. "Here, have a seat."

Abby sat on one end of the long couch and accepted the glass he offered. She sipped her wine and thought to herself how different the two brothers were. But in some ways there was a similarity, something she couldn't quite put her finger on—yet.

J.R. leaned back at the opposite end of the couch, watching Abby and cradling his drink.

"Okay, let's get down to business. You said something about my brother on the phone. What is it?"

Abby wove the story of Gary's financial need in a carefully constructed series of half truths and omissions. She had to play her cards close to her chest until she found out where she and Gary stood with J.R. She never really lied to J.R., but she gave incomplete facts so as to prevent the truth from surfacing and destroying her chances of winning his respect.

She'd just about finished when he cut in. "Are you telling me my brother sent you to ask me for fifty thousand dollars?"

She shook her head. "No, Gary didn't send me. He doesn't know I've come and neither does *my* brother."

"It's so hard to keep these brothers straight."

"Try. It's important."

But J.R. was far more interested in the way her blue dress slipped up around her knees when she crossed her legs than any deal she was trying to discuss with him. The long, shapely legs were difficult not to notice and admire.

Shifting slightly, Abby let the skirt climb a little higher on her thin, attractive thighs, knowing she had his attention. "You see, Sid—"

"Your brother."

"Yes. Sid's business is having problems. Gary worked out a very clever plan that could—"

"Gary's a clever boy," J.R. interjected with a smile that didn't touch his eyes.

"Yes, he is, and he's got a chance to buy a warehouse full of—"

"So he needs money," J.R. cut in. The lady was beating around the bush and he was bored with it. Watching her on the couch, he felt his senses come alive. He was here in Knots Landing, alone with a beautiful woman. "Tell me something," he murmured, loosening his tie. "I'm sure you'll forgive my naivete, but if Gary is such a clever boy, why doesn't he just go to a bank for this money?"

Caught off guard, Abby hesitated. "Actually, he did," she lied, taking a sip of wine. "They turned him down."

He saw through her charade and laughed. "I guess Gary's credit's about as good as it's ever been."

Leaning her head back on the couch, Abby decided to play a waiting game.

J.R. sipped at his drink and studied her, the way she moved her head against the leather, her wide, sensuous blue eyes as they stared at him. He felt hot, uncomfortable. Her smooth, sculpted curves were damned inviting, and the neckline of her silk dress dipped low enough to offer him just a glimpse of her tanned skin. He slid a little closer to her and his fingers touched her shoulder. "Forgive me, but you are an unusually attractive woman."

"Thank you."

"And an altruistic one—coming to me to help my brother to help your brother. . . ." His fingers began moving gently against the silk, sliding it across her shoulder.

"I believe in families helping one another," she whispered.

"Now, I believe the very same thing. 'Course

then again they've got to be *talkin'* to one another before they can help one another. And as far as I can recall Gary's not talkin' to me these days." He studied the pout of her lips, the way her golden curls strayed around her face.

"Suppose he came to you himself," Abby suggested. "Would you help him then?"

"I might be disposed," he agreed, his eyes a smoldering dark blue. "We'd have to cap that well when we came to it, though, wouldn't we?"

"I could get Gary to talk to you."

"Could you now?" His fingers touched her neck.

"I think so."

"I think so, too. If a brother of mine wanted to sit down with me, I'd be delighted to meet him."

"He'll be here," she said.

"You're mighty sure of yourself, aren't you?"

She looked down at his hand and offered a vague smile.

J.R. helped her to her feet, still touching her, still staring into her eyes. But his gaze had changed slightly. The sparks of desire still lingered in its clear blue depth, but they were tempered with a new respect. "You know, I've got a notion if you work on him like you worked on me, you might just be right about that."

"I'll talk to him soon."

"Good. Then we'll meet again. Tomorrow night?"

Abby lifted her chin. "Tomorrow's fine."

"How about that restaurant near the beach. What was the name of it?"

"Sterlings?"

J.R. grinned. "That's the one. I'll be there around seven," he said, walking her to the door, his eyes watching her every move.

"Seven at Sterlings," she said with a smile as she walked back into the hall and heard the door shut behind her.

I wouldn't miss it for the world! she thought.

"So far, so good," Abby told herself as she parked her car in her usual spot at Knots Landing Motors, hurried inside and discovered that Gary was in his office. "Great, here goes nothing," she said to herself. Pasting on a bright smile, she walked into the small office and closed the door behind her.

Gary looked up from the paperwork on his desk and knew by the gleam in her eye that something was up. "What's going on?"

She sat on the corner of his desk, letting her skirt hike up her leg. "I've found a solution to our problem."

"Our problem," he repeated, his eyes narrowing suspiciously.

"With Frank and Roy and the Orchid Cab Company."

"Oh, *that* problem." He leaned back in his chair and toyed with a pencil. "What did you do?"

She smiled. "Just ran into your brother. He's in town, you know."

"You *what* ?"

"I saw J.R. and asked him to help us out!"

The pencil between Gary's fingers snapped into two jagged pieces, and in her mind Abby saw her idea going up in smoke.

"*No* !"

"But, Gary—"

"I said *no*." He was yelling so loudly that his words echoed down the halls of the office area.

"But fifty thousand dollars doesn't mean a thing to him. He'll help. I'm sure of it." But Abby's words seemed to touch an already raw nerve.

"You're sure. Terrific."

"Absolutely," Abby confirmed.

He tried to read the expression on her face. She looked like the cat that had swallowed the canary. Obviously something was going on behind his back, and he wanted it out in the open. She was leaning forward, and he took advantage of it by grabbing her wrist. "Okay, Abby, just what the hell did you do?"

"Nothing . . . I just bumped into him."

"Nobody bumps into J.R." His grip tightened, and he pushed his face so close to hers that she could almost feel the anger burning in his eyes.

"I was curious about him. So I went to the hotel."

"Oh, no."

She shrugged and attempted to soften the picture that was forming in his mind. "I hung around the coffee shop till he showed up."

"J.R. doesn't do coffee shops, Abby."

"Right. But as long as I was there—"

"I don't believe this." Gary let her go, and grabbing his jacket, strode out of his office. He wanted to turn his back on this whole ridiculous affair. Frank, Roy, Sid, Abby, and now J.R.

Where would it all end? Right now, he hated himself for his impulsive greed. Cursing loudly, he stomped down the stairway.

"Gary, be reasonable," she pleaded as she followed him.

"There is no way I'm going to ask my brother for money."

"It's business, Gary. It's not personal."

"With my family? It's personal!"

She grabbed his arm and jerked him to the side of the hall, out of hearing range of two salesmen walking past. "There's a lot at stake here, Gary. You contracted for those parts."

"There's no contract."

"Roy Lance and Frank Korshak think you've got a contract."

"Well, I don't."

"But they say you do and they'll enforce it!" she whispered, wishing she could talk some sense into him. Then she glanced around, hoping that no one in the office had overheard the conversation. If Sid found out what was happening, he'd be furious. "Those guys from the Orchid Cab Company; they don't fool around."

"Oh, come on! What do you think they're going to do? Break my fingers?"

"Or worse," she murmured, running her fingers nervously through her hair. "You've only got a couple of days—maybe a week—and then they'll be back!"

Gary considered the irony of it. "What a choice . . . those goons, or my brother the goon." Turning away from Abby, he cursed the situation. "So now I'm between a rock and a hard place." But he was weakening, and he hated himself for it.

Abby, seeing him softening, played her trump card. "Gary, you've got to think about Sid, too. And the business."

"Sid? Sid's against the idea. He doesn't want to have anything to do with stolen parts."

"Of course he doesn't! But he still needs them."

Placing his hands on her shoulders, he looked her straight in the eye. "There's something you have to understand: all my life, every time I've tangled with my older brother, I've lost."

"What about last year, when he came looking for oil off Knots Landing Beach? I hear you stopped him cold."

Gary's lips twisted cynically. "Yeah, I stopped him. And two minutes after we won, J.R. had everything turned around to his own advantage. He was on the cover of *Time* magazine."

"So what? That's the way things should be in business. Everybody wins. It's exciting. And it's exactly what can happen now."

"Wrong! Abby, when my brother wins, everybody else loses. If you fool around with him long enough, you're going to find that out."

"Just meet with him, Gary," she pleaded desperately. As she saw it, J.R. was his only hope. *Her* only hope.

The hallway was suddenly deathly quiet. She took hold of his hands, begged him with her eyes, silently coaxed him to take what was being offered. He stood motionless, thinking about all the unpleasant possibilities and searching for an answer he could live with.

"Please," she whispered.

Slowly, he let his hands drop. "*No*!" His jaw jutted with renewed determination as he turned and walked away.

Watching him stride out the front door, she balled a fist and promised herself that she'd find a way to save them both. And, whether Gary Ewing liked it or not, his only salvation was his brother.

Richard Avery was in a bad mood. The last couple of days, ever since that pain of a husband of hers brought the kids home, Abby had been cool. It was maddening seeing her irritation whenever he knocked on her door.

To make matters worse, Laura was so wrapped up in her work that she barely noticed him. All she did was work, work, work—rubbing Richard's nose in the fact that he was no longer the primary breadwinner of the family. Big deal.

Still angry, he walked into the kitchen to make himself a sandwich. Laura was in the family room, banging on her damned calculator and doing whatever it was she thought was so all-fired important. The continual clicking of the keys got under his skin.

"Laura!" he yelled, trying to get her attention. "The hot mustard, Laura. Where's the hot mustard?"

Distracted, she looked up. "In the cupboard

next to the stove. Second shelf."

Finding it there, Richard turned his attention and frustration to the next item on his menu. "Pumpernickel?" he yelled.

"In the refrigerator."

"I know that. *Where* in the refrigerator?"

"I don't know exactly. Look around." She felt the tension in the room but tried to concentrate on her work, pounding out the numbers to determine the amortization schedule on her latest real estate deal.

"Jesus! Who wrapped it in foil?" he exclaimed, making her hit the wrong key and lose her calculations.

"You're the only one who eats it," she muttered under her breath as the calculator jammed.

"So where'd you hide the Bermuda onions?"

She tossed her notebook onto the couch and let the calculator fall to the floor. "I'll make your sandwich, if it's such a problem."

"I can do it."

"Really. I don't mind." Her teeth clenched, she walked over to the refrigerator, grabbed the bread and began slapping mustard on two slices.

Richard took the knife from her and pointed the dull blade at her face. "I'm trying to make a sandwich and you're treating me like a five-year-old."

"That's not true."

"It sure as hell is! It's been happening ever since I lost my job and you became such a hotshot in the real estate business. It's patronizing and condescending and I don't like it."

She felt tears sting the back of her eyes, and her shoulders slumped. "Richard, that's so unfair. I've never done anything but try to make things easier for you."

"Yeah, well do me a favor then."

"What?" she asked, meeting the anger in his glare.

"Stop trying to make it easier. Just go out and convert condos or clear escrow. I'll take care of myself." With his biting words still ringing in the air, he stomped out of the room.

Quivering inside, she returned to the couch and looked at the mess of paperwork on the floor. Ignoring it, she sat on the edge of one of the cushions and tried to sort out her feelings. Her husband was being totally irrational, and she didn't know how to begin to solve their problems. She only felt pressure and anxiety building between them every day.

Cradling her head in her hands, she started to cry. Confused and hurt, she tried not to think about Richard's cruelty, or the vase of tiny yellow roses still sitting in her office.

Michael Fairgate sat at the dining room table, thoroughly engrossed in his project. He was cutting pictures from books and magazines and arranging them around the work area. His movements were very erratic, quick and somewhat clumsy. The effects of his hyperkinesis produced numerous spills, jagged cuts, and in general, sloppy work, but he was proud of himself. He heard his mother banging around in the kitchen and barely noticed when his older sister, Diana, entered the room.

Throwing an arm around his shoulder, she looked at his work. "What are you making, Michael?"

"A project for school. It's a collage," he said with a grin.

Diana surveyed his efforts and nodded. "Nice work—" she began, but before she could finish her thought, her eyes focused on her green album and her stomach dropped to the floor. For a minute she couldn't believe her eyes, wouldn't accept the fact that her brother could be so stupid. "Michael! That's my school yearbook!"

He hurriedly threw a magazine over the book in an attempt to hide it. Diana reached over, grabbed the glossy magazine and tossed it on the floor. Her eyes widened in horror as she turned the mutilated pages of her annual. Her voice was shaking. "This is very precious to me, Michael . . . and you've cut it to shreds."

"But I needed pictures of a basketball game."

"You had no right to go into my room and steal my things!"

Karen, having heard the screams, entered the room and attempted to restore order. "A little louder—they can't hear you at the Ward house!"

Diana turned her furious gaze on her mother. "Mom, Michael stole my year book—"

"I didn't steal it. I borrowed it."

"And you ruined it!"

"Wait a minute, wait a minute. Time out!" Karen surveyed the damage and shook her head. "Michael, that wasn't the best idea you ever had."

He swallowed hard. "I'm sorry, Mom."

"I know, sweetheart." Pulling Diana into the kitchen, Karen tried to smooth her daughter's ruffled feathers. "He hasn't used the pictures yet. Maybe you can paste them back in."

"That's not going to help! He wrecked it!"

Karen pushed a wayward lock of Diana's hair from her face. "I know, sweetie, but . . . after all that Michael's been through, we don't want to make things any harder on him than they have to be. Look how quietly and well he's working."

Still furious, Diana jerked away and sat down at the kitchen table. From her position she could look through the door and see Michael and her yearbook, her precious cut-up yearbook. Michael looked into the kitchen but quickly turned away. Diana leveled indignant eyes on her mother. "How can you take his side?" she demanded, her face flushed with anger. "If I did what he did, you'd have my head."

Karen tried to remain calm. Struggling with Michael's illness had been hard on all of them, but he'd made progress—tremendous progress. They couldn't stop now. "Diana, we all promised to make an extra effort with Michael—"

"I can't believe it! He takes my things, and I'm the one who gets yelled at!" Storming out of the room, she slammed the kitchen door behind her and stomped up the stairs.

With a sigh, Karen walked back into the dining room, stood behind her son, and with lines of worry etching her brow, watched over his shoulder. Smiling as she tousled his hair, she looked at his work and felt a sense of pride at the concentration he was putting into it. "I think it would be better if you didn't take your sister's things without her permission," she suggested. "Okay?"

"Okay, Mom," he whispered. "I didn't mean to do it."

"What is this you're working on, anyway?" She lifted up the construction paper and looked with a critical eye at the pictures pasted haphazardly.

Bright and bubbling again, he said, "A collage for school."

"Sweetie, that's wonderful! Need any help?"

"No, I can do it—"

But without even realizing what she was doing, Karen started to straighten up the mess he had made. In her own way, she was always trying to protect him from the cruelty of the world.

As Abby approached the exclusive westside restaurant that J.R. had selected, she thought to herself that this was how diplomats must feel about political negotiations. Shuttling back and forth between two warring factions. Trying to get one side to sit down and talk to the other. Never promising to either side more than one could deliver.

She had known that Gary was going to be hard to convince, but he was putting up a stronger fight than she had anticipated. Now she felt a little embarrassed going back to J.R. after she had assured him that she could get Gary to cooperate.

J.R. hadn't seemed surprised when she had

phoned to inform him of the impasse she had reached with Gary. However, he'd suggested that they have dinner together anyway, and she had leaped at the chance to see him again. She wasn't about to let Gary's foolish pride ruin everything for the both of them. J.R. could help them—would help them. If only Gary would quit being so bull-headed!

Tossing her hair, she opened the door of the restaurant, smoothed her dress and walked to the maître d'.

"Mr. Ewing?" the small man inquired and nodded quickly. "Ah, yes. Follow me, please."

Abby noted the bone-white walls, the dimmed, cut-glass chandeliers, and the white lace and linen on the tables, as well as the freshly cut flowers and flickering candles. She could feel the intimacy of the room, the excitement of meeting J.R. in such private surroundings. Sensing the eyes of the other patrons watching her, she glided between the tables, and felt more alive than she had in years. She knew she looked her best; she could feel her burgundy dress cling in the right places and swirl about her legs.

The maître d' led her to a private alcove with a magnificent view of the ocean. A bottle of champagne had already been opened and was sitting in a silver bucket. J.R. was studying the view when she entered. He rose from the table to greet her with a finger to his lips to prevent her from talking.

"Now, now, luscious lady, don't even try to apologize for my family's bad manners."

He waved the waiter away. "We just need a

few minutes alone," he said, winking to the man who quietly exited.

Then, with Texan charm oozing out of him, he seated Abby next to him at the table and sat down himself, so close that he could see the streaks of green in her beautiful blue eyes. "Seems to me you're working awful hard for a man who doesn't want to be helped," he observed.

"Gary needs to be helped," she said.

J.R. shook his head. "He needs to be nursed, maybe . . . maybe whipped." He chuckled to himself. "You gonna do those things for him?"

She refused to reply, playing along with his game.

He poured them each a glass of champagne. As he sipped his, he watched her over the rim of his glass. "Now suppose the gentleman did manage to extend himself and come ask me for that money? What benefit—apart from the joys of brotherly affection—would I be able to gain from the transaction?"

Caught off guard for a split second, Abby felt her heart begin to race. "There's the interest on the money . . ."

He roared with laughter. "On fifty thousand dollars? Oh, I do like you! Honey, that wouldn't be enough to pay for a year's worth of my boot shines."

Abby knew how to hit him close to home. "There is another thing. You know Valene's been talking about moving back to Dallas . . ."

J.R. didn't move. "Is that so?"

"Well, if Gary fails at Knots Landing Motors, it'll be hard to persuade her he's got anything here to stay for. So I suppose they'll go back.'' She shrugged, smiled, and sipped her champagne.

"To Dallas . . .'' he murmured.

Setting the hook deeper, she continued, ''She misses Lucy so much. I guess if Gary fails here, he'll go back to work with your company.''

His eyes sharpened. ''That'd be fun. Is that woman really trying to get him back there?''

Now reeling in her catch, she finished him off, ''It's all she ever talks about. But with fifty thousand dollars he could make a success of himself right here in Knots Landing.''

He leaned back in his chair to scrutinize her. Was she telling him the truth or only manipulating him? He couldn't be sure. What were her motivations in this game? He didn't have any answers but he did enjoy the questions. Looking at her again, he had to admit that she would be a fine asset to a busy man like himself back in Dallas.

''You're a wickedly clever lady, Miss Abby. I can't say I'm sure I believe what you're saying . . . but maybe it doesn't matter. All right. I'll make it easier, but he's got to ask me himself for that loan. Now how are you gonna get him to do that?''

Abby pondered carefully. ''Well, if Muhammad won't go to the mountain . . .''

Picking up the thought, he grinned devilishly. ''You want the mountain to . . .''

''. . . go to Muhammad.''

J.R. chuckled. ''Why not?'' He glanced through the windows to the vibrant sunset on the beach—the beach where he'd lost millions because Gary had publicly stood up to him and

fought the Petrolux off-shore drilling at Knots
Landing.

Well, now the tables had turned!

"More champagne?" he asked his beautiful
guest. Yes, sir, things in Knots Landing were
definitely looking up!

Chapter Four

When the Mountain Meets Muhammed

Gary Ewing's day wasn't going well. Actually, he thought cynically, the entire *week* had been a disaster.

Val had been cool, almost suspicious, ever since he'd come home with that stupid story about the box of transmission housings being the cause of his bruises.

To make matters worse, J.R. was back in town.

Grimacing, Gary leaned his hip against the door of a blue convertible and looked around the showroom. A few customers wandered between the shiny new models, but he was trapped on the floor with an old geezer who had a hearing problem and didn't really seem interested in buying; the gray-haired man was just ambling aimlessly around the showroom and looking at each car. He would run his hands along the sleek fenders, sit in the plush seats, and study the interiors, but all in all, he was just killing an afternoon—and wasting Gary's time.

He should have pushed the sale, but didn't. His mind kept wandering to the terrifying mess his life had become. He knew his time was running out. Frank and Roy were sure to be back any day. He could only guess how far they were willing to go to carry out their threats.

Then there was good ol' J.R. The fact that he was back in Knots Landing made Gary nervous—very nervous. What had possessed Abby to see him? Involving J.R. in the Orchid Cab mess was a mistake. Wherever he went, trouble was soon to follow. And there was trouble in Knots Landing. Gary could feel it.

Pacing around like a caged tiger, he was so deep in worry that he didn't notice that just outside the showroom window a long silver limousine had pulled up to the curb. As it idled in the shade of the palms, a tall man in a wide-brimmed Stetson opened the back door, swiped at a speck of dust on his snakeskin boots, and climbed out.

Inside the showroom Gary concentrated on the most pressing of his problems: where he was going to come up with fifty thousand dollars. Maybe he could still talk Frank and Roy out of the deal if he couldn't raise the money—

"This damn thing ain't worth two cents!" the old man shouted as he leaned against a bright yellow sports car.

Gary's concentration snapped. "What—?"

"I keep telling my wife it don't do me no good."

Gary, brought back to reality by the loud

voice, watched as the man tapped the side of his head. Then, grinning, he realized that the elderly customer was rambling on about his hearing aid.

"Hello, Gary."

The familiar Texan drawl caught him off guard. Memories flooded through him like tidal wave and his gut wrenched. J.R. was back in his life!

Oblivious to the small drama going on around him, the old man continued muttering as he opened and slammed the door of the sports car. "Ain't like fifteen, twenty years ago, I can tell you. Cars were made solid then . . ."

But Gary's attention was solely on J.R. "What are you doing here?"

J.R. flashed him a broad, friendly smile. "Well, I'm in L.A. for a day or two and I wasn't about to leave without stopping in to see my brother."

"Nice of you," Gary said, his every word as cold as ice.

The old man cut in. "Look, I ain't sure about this car. I'll come back with the wife—"

"Good idea," Gary said, his eyes riveted to J.R. In his peripheral vision he saw the customer shuffle out of the show room, and didn't care that he might have lost a potential sale.

He tensed for the inevitable battle. Like two similarly charged magnets, J.R. and Gary had always pushed each other away. And today, Gary was spoiling for a fight. "I don't buy the concerned-big-brother bit."

"Well, now—"

Abby rushed into the room. She'd seen the limo, known that J.R. had landed, and sensing the confrontation about to take place, hurried into the showroom to take control.

"Mr. Ewing!" she called, breathless by the time she reached J.R. Despite the fact that her nerves were stretched tighter than piano wire, she managed a smile. "Well, how are you?"

He looked at her, smiled and then bowed slightly, "Hello there . . ."

"What a nice surprise!"

Gary thought he would be sick. Abby and her schemes!

Linking her arm through Gary's, she pulled him close to her and ignored the fury burning in his eyes. Then she latched on to J.R. and led them both toward the back of the showroom, to the door leading to the garage. "Come on, Gary, let's show your brother around," she suggested.

J.R. glanced at his brother and his blue eyes gleamed. "I hear you're building a real nice life out here for yourself, Gary."

Boiling inside, Gary held his tongue.

Abby knew he was going to blow the whole deal. Stifling the urge to kick him, she tossed her hair over her shoulder and beamed at J.R. "He certainly is."

J.R. gave a curt nod. He was a master at sticking pins in all the right places and twisting them at just the right time. And he loved to bait his younger brother. "So, you're laying in roots . . . on the wagon, too. And from what I heard you practically rebuilt this company."

"No, that's not true—"

"And that stuff's nothing to sneeze about, Gary."

"I didn't rebuild this company!"

Slapping him on the back, J.R. laughed. "I can see you haven't lost any of that modesty. Come on, boy, you're a Ewing. You ought to let these people out here know it."

Abby nudged Gary but didn't say anything. The wrong word right now would send him into a rage. Then they'd both lose their shot at J.R.'s fifty grand, the money that might just save their necks.

They approached the garage and J.R. held open the door as Abby and Gary stepped through. The noise inside was deafening, and the dark interior smelled of oil and grease.

Abby wrinkled her nose, but plunged on, looking for her brother. Sid always could smooth things over; maybe just talking with him would calm Gary down.

Sid was busy working on the pistons of a radically new car engine he'd designed. The three of them came up to him. His mouth tightened for a minute when he recognized J.R., but he mentally forced himself to put the past to rest. What had happened with Petrolux and J.R. was long over, and Karen had won. He straightened and wiped the grease from his fingers before extending his hand.

"Well, look who's back in town," he shouted over the high-powered whine of the engine.

"Glad to see ya, Sid—"

Seeing his chance to talk with Abby alone, Gary pulled her over to the side of the shop, away from J.R.'s ears and the roar of the experimental engine. "What the hell did you bring him here for?"

"You need him, Gary."

"Like I need a hole in my head. Abby, you don't know what you're getting into—"

"He can do you a lot of good. Trust me," she said, jerking her arm free and starting back to the others, but she felt her confidence begin to flag under Gary's accusing stare.

J.R. pushed his hands into his pockets and rocked back on his heels as he looked around the busy service department. Men in blue uniforms were hard at work on various cars. The clanking of tools and the roar of engines nearly drowned the sound of a country-western tune on the intercom.

"Hell of an operation you've got here, Sid," J.R. observed, his eyes roving over the beehive of activity.

"We're proud of it."

"Yes, sir. It's almost big enough to qualify for a Texas franchise." Sid and Abby laughed, but the sound could scarcely be heard over the noise. "Why don't you turn that thing off, Sid?"

"Good idea." Sid killed the engine, and a more moderate level of background noise remained.

The heavy smell of gas and the choking effect of the exhaust smoke made it hard to breathe, but J.R. found it comfortable; watching so many people working always made him feel good. He grinned at Sid. "Doing your own repair work?"

Sid chuckled. "No, this is an engine I'm designing."

"You don't say."

Abby filled him in on the details. "Sid's been working on it for years. It's going to get a hundred miles to a gallon of gas."

"Now, hold on! You'll put me out of the oil business!"

Sid smiled, but deep furrows etched his brow. "I'm afraid it'll be a while before the kinks are worked out of it."

Gary watched his brother as J.R. turned his attention directly on the engine and studied it with a greedy glint in his eyes. The muscles in Gary's neck began to ache, and he felt the same old premonition of dread he always did when J.R. wanted something. Damn it all, he should never have let J.R. in here!

"I do admire people who can design things like that. That's a talent I stand in awe of. You must have a dozen patents on that already," J.R. said, pointing at the motor.

Sid shook his head. "It's not exactly at that point yet."

"No?" J.R. tried to conceal his surprise at this news, but a hint of something malicious crept into his expression.

"Maybe we should leave," Gary cut in.

But J.R. wouldn't hear of it. He knew that this engine was something he would have to learn more about. He had a gut feeling that it just might benefit him. "Not quite yet, Gary. I'm mighty interested in this here motor—"

"It looks more complete than it is," Sid said warily.

"Now *he's* being modest," Abby said, winking broadly at her brother.

"I'd sure like to hear more about that," J.R.

said, tapping the manifold. "Yes, sir. I really would."

Sensing an opening that would assist in her plans, Abby placed her hand on J.R.'s sleeve. "Hey, I've got an idea—"

A sudden blast from the intercom cut her short. "Mr. Fairgate . . . you're wanted in the showroom, please . . . Mr. Fairgate."

"Sorry," Sid said, glancing from J.R. to Gary and then back again. "But duty calls." He gave an exasperated shrug and started out of the shop area, but Abby stopped him with a hand on his arm.

"Wait, Sid. Look, J.R.'s only in town for another day or so. How about you all coming over to my house for dinner tonight? We'll be able to relax and talk."

Gary felt as if he'd been trapped by Abby and J.R. Scrambling for an escape, he shot her a killing glance and rubbed his hand over his tense neck muscles. "I don't think that's a good idea. Val and I are busy—"

"Oh, come on, now, Gary. I'm only going to be in town for a few days. You can change your plans for one night," J.R. cut in.

Abby wouldn't let anyone beg off. "I'll talk to Val, Gary. What about you, Sid?"

"Well, I'll have to check with Karen."

"I already talked to her. So it will be Sid and Karen, J.R., Gary, Val . . ."

Gary frowned, his eyes narrowing on Abby. "I don't know about us."

J.R. cleared his throat and mustered as much sincerity as possible. "Come on, now. It's been a long time since we broke bread together."

"I know Val will want to say hello," Abby said.

About as much as she'd like to dine with a cobra, Gary thought, frowning at Abby. He looked back at his brother's arrogant face.

"Yeah, it'll be real nice to see her," J.R. decided.

The intercom came back on line, and this time Sid took off, agreeing to see them all later at dinner. He looked one last time over his shoulder and told himself that he was being overly suspicious. But it still bothered him, the way that J.R. had studied his engine with his intense blue eyes. The Texan looked just like a cat who'd stumbled onto a crippled bird. Trying to shake the feeling, Sid half ran to the showroom.

The muscles in Gary's jaw tightened. "Val might have plans."

"Nonsense," Abby said with a grin. "Besides, she'll change them for a chance to see her brother-in-law again. Now, come on, it's all settled! It'll be my first real dinner party!"

Feeling as if his entire world were teetering on the edge of a ravine, Gary gritted his teeth and, without a word of good-bye, headed back to the showroom. With any luck, Val would have a good excuse not to go to the fiasco that Abby was cooking up.

Karen parked her car in the driveway near the back door. With a frown, she looked at the overflowing sacks of groceries sitting on the floor of the car. "No time like the present, I

suppose,'' she said to herself as she got out of
the car and grabbed two of the heaviest bags.

As Karen was juggling the bags, Ginger
walked up the Fairgate driveway. ''Need a
hand?'' she asked, helping Karen as the bottom
of one sack gave out.

''Looks like I do need one,'' Karen replied.

''Or two or three . . .''

Laughing, Karen unlocked the back door and
Ginger brought in two more sacks. She'd been
weeding the flower beds, waiting anxiously
for Karen to return. She needed to talk to
someone . . . anyone. Anyone, that is, except
Kenny.

Karen, staggering under the ungainly load,
managed to lug the bags into the kitchen and
set them on the counter. Ginger went to the
window and stared outside to the climbing rose
on Karen's trellis.

''Thanks. I sure needed that extra pair of
arms,'' she said as she began to put vegetables
into the refrigerator.

''Anytime.'' Ginger bit her lower lip and
looked at her friend. ''Besides, I wanted to talk
to you.''

''Great! Hold on a minute, and I'll get us
some iced tea.'' Karen poured them each a
glass and then frowned at the broken sack.
Canned and dried foods were spilling onto the
counter. ''I cleaned out the health food store.
Michael's on a special diet, you know.''

Fidgeting, Ginger tried to sound interested.
''That's right, and how is he doing?''

''Oh, much better. The institute that was recommended to us has just been fantastic!''

Karen squeezed some lemon into a glass of iced tea and then passed it.

"I'm really glad for you," Ginger murmured. She was nearly bursting inside with her own worries, but she took a sip of tea and then hoisted another bag from the table over to the counter. "Say, what's in this bag? It's really heavy."

"Enough dried beans to choke a horse." Karen stopped putting things away and turned to her friend. For the first time, she noticed the worry in her large eyes, and that her tanned skin was unnaturally pale. "Now, tell me, what about you? What did you want to talk about?"

Ginger couldn't meet her gaze.

"Well?"

Drawing in a large breath, Ginger searched the ceiling with her eyes. "I'm pregnant!"

Karen, caught off guard for a minute, didn't say a word. Then she threw her arms around her friend and beamed, though she felt on the verge of tears. "Ginger, that's wonderful! What a dope I've been, rattling on about these stupid groceries. Now, come on, tell me all about it!"

"Well . . ." Ginger blinked back her own tears.

"It is good news, isn't it?"

"It would have been—last year. This year, I don't know. I'm so confused."

"Have you talked to Kenny about it?"

"Not yet," Ginger admitted, pushing her red hair away from her face and trying to keep her voice even.

"Why not?"

"Oh, Karen," she said with a sigh. Looking

through the window again, she swallowed hard. "If Kenny and I can't work things out, having a baby isn't going to make any difference."

"But you have to talk to him about it."

"I know, but I'm afraid to. I'm afraid of what he'll say . . . or won't say . . ."

Diana pushed open the kitchen door. Dressed in a sloppy sweatshirt and jeans, she eyed her mother and Ginger, ignored the obvious fact that she'd just walked in on a personal conversation, dropped into one of the chairs at the table and licked an ice cream cone.

Karen was perturbed by Diana's intrusion, and by the ice cream cone. "Where'd you get that?" she asked.

"I made it." Still simmering from the argument with her mother a few days earlier, Diana picked up a box of granola, and wrinkled her nose at the package. "Health food. Ugh!" Slouching lower in the chair, she gazed at Karen with bored defiance.

"You made it?" Karen repeated, walking to the table. "With what?"

"I brought home some ice cream. It's in the freezer." Her voice had a cutting edge, as if she were daring Karen.

"I thought I told you I don't want foods like that in the house. Suppose Michael comes in?"

"So?"

Karen felt her jaw tighten. "It's not on his diet, and it makes it harder for him if he sees us eating the foods he's not allowed to have."

"Michael, Michael, Michael!" Diana exploded, ignoring the fact that her ice cream was melting and dripping onto the table. "I'm sick and tired of hearing about Michael!"

"All I'm asking for is a little cooperation!"

Diana scraped her chair back and, casting her mother a furious glance, started out of the room.

"And I don't like you always walking out when I'm talking to you!" Karen yelled, losing all control.

"Why not?" she threw back, not bothering to hide her sarcasm. "It will give you more time to think about Michael!" With that parting shot, she ran out the back door, flipped the remainder of her cone into the flower bed, and took off on her ten-speed.

"Great," Karen muttered, grabbing a towel and wiping the ice cream from the table.

Ginger saw the defeated look on her face. "I'm sorry. It looks like you have enough troubles without mine to listen to."

"It's okay," she said, offering Ginger a sad smile. But she almost had to agree with her friend. The problems she was having with her children, the pressure on Sid at work, Jeff and Abby bickering and fighting, everything happening at once! Where were the good old days of peace and quiet and her normal, happy life?

"I think I'd better go—"

"No, that's all right. I have great answers for other people's problems. It's only my own I have a hard time with." She stared absently after the departed Diana and wondered to herself if she could hold everything together. She'd felt the tension building in Sid over problems with the business as well as Michael's

health and its effects on the family. Diana's
eruptions were becoming more and more fre-
quent. And poor Eric—he seemed to have gotten lost in the shuffle. Combined, the entire
Fairgate family was a powder keg, ready to
explode. "Come on, have another glass of tea
and let's talk about that baby of yours!".

Without waiting for Ginger's response, she
tossed the dirty towel into the sink, poured them
each another glass of tea and forced Ginger to sit
at the table. "Now, what're you going to do?"

As Gary Ewing drove home from work, his
mind retraced the events of the past few days,
wondering where everything would lead. Grip-
ping the wheel of the truck more tightly, he
came to the conclusion that he'd have to deal
with Frank and Roy again very soon. "What I
need now is a miracle," he told himself with a
wry smile. "And the only miracle left is good
ol' J.R.! Damn!"

He rolled down the window and swore
again. J.R., miracle or not, wasn't someone he
could trust. Abby could preach all she wanted,
but Gary knew how the sermon would end.

As traffic slowed, Gary shifted down. The cab
of the pickup was sweltering hot. He didn't
really care. All he could think of was J.R. and
the goons from the Orchid Cab Company.

"You're an idiot," he told himself, switching
on the radio. "You should never, *never* have
gotten involved with those creeps!" He thought
about stopping off for a drink but didn't. Turning to the bottle again would only make things
worse.

He punched the buttons of the radio. Traffic reports, interrupted only sporadically by music, blared across the airwaves of every station.

L.A.—Ain't it great, Gary thought as the pickup crept along at a snail's pace. Honking horns had become part of the normal background noise of everyday life. Oppressive heat and yellow-brown smog seemed to continually climb from the horizon. It was a picture of discord, dirt and depression—and, Gary thought cynically, it was the picture of his life.

When he finally pulled into his driveway, Gary knew that news of the dinner party at Abby's was going to be as welcome to Valene as a nest of termites. Abby and J.R. both represented direct threats to her home, particularly J.R. Val had never forgiven J.R. for his role in separating her from Lucy, and she had never liked the way that he treated Gary.

He jerked the keys out of the ignition and stuffed them into his pocket. *It's now or never*, he told himself as he got out of the pickup and decided to break the news to Val the minute he walked through the door.

"I just can't believe you agreed to it!" Val exclaimed, pacing from one end of the living room to the other. "Abby and J.R.! Good Lord, Gary, what got into you?"

With his feet up on the couch and his head propped back against the cushions, Gary had listened to her blow off steam for twenty minutes. The damned thing of it was that he couldn't even argue with her.

"Okay, Val, okay. Look, it wasn't my idea.

I don't want to go, either, but—''

''Well, then it's simple. You don't want to go. I don't want to go. We won't go. Okay?''

The doorbell rang sharply before he could reply.

''I'll get it!'' she said, stomping over to the door and pulling it open.

Karen was on the front porch. She held a chicken leg in her hand and was munching away on it. ''Hi.''

Gary and Val were surprised and confused, but some of the fury in their argument disappeared at the comical sight.

''Karen?'' Val said, looking quizzically at the chicken leg and laughing. ''What's going on?''

''Abby just called me. Dinner's going to be a half an hour late,'' Karen said. Watching the couple exchange glances, she pursed her lips. ''You're not going?''

Defiantly, Val crossed her arms over her chest. ''No. We're not!''

''Come on, Val,'' Karen prodded. ''Nobody can stand J.R.! That's why he's such fun. It's not like last year. He doesn't want anything from us now!''

''Don't bet on that,'' Val muttered, eyeing her husband.

Gary looked away, inadvertently rubbing his shoulder—the shoulder Roy had slammed against the wall only a few days before.

Karen wagged her chicken bone at Valene. ''Oh, come on, you guys. Besides, this is Abby's first dinner party. Can you imagine what we're going to get to eat? French fries, hot dogs . . . better eat something now, then you won't be hungry later."

Val chuckled in spite of herself.

"I knew I could get you to change your mind," Karen said. Still laughing, she held up her chicken leg and took a large bite before waving good-bye and heading back home.

"See, it won't be so bad," Gary said. He walked over to Val, placed his hands on her waist.

"You don't know that," she whispered, holding her husband close. "And with Abby and J.R., I feel like there's gonna be trouble. Terrible trouble."

"You worry too much," he said, kissing her gently on her forehead.

"Only about us. You and me . . . and Lucy. J.R. hurt us once before; he'll do it again, Gary. I just know it."

His arms tightened around Valene's soft body. He breathed in the scent of her hair, felt her skin warm beneath his hands. He'd failed her once before, long ago, and he vowed to himself that he'd never let it happen again.

Abby was busy in her dining room, arranging bone china and champagne glasses on her favorite linen tablecloth. Everything was perfect! The sterling silver was polished, its bright patina reflecting the light from the chandelier. Cut flowers floating in a crystal bowl and tapered candles in silver candlesticks added just the right touch of color and fragrance to the room.

She could hardly wait. She'd worked hard to bring all the elements together. Now she was going to make sure that the setting was just right.

Crossing her fingers, she hoped that everything would go as planned. If only Gary wasn't so bull-headed about his brother. If only he could see that everything was going to be okay and that J.R. wasn't going to threaten anything or anyone. If only he would see how much they needed J.R. and his money.

Still stuffing the mauve napkins into the empty glasses, she looked up and caught Olivia hanging around by the doorway. She chewed her lip nervously and avoided Abby's eyes.

"Mom, I'm not hungry," she said.

"What's the matter, sweetheart?"

"I think I'm upset."

"About what?" Abby straightened, eyed the table one more time and turned all of her attention on her daughter.

Olivia's eyes wandered around the room for a minute and her fingers slid nervously on the door frame. "Do you think we're happy? Me and Brian, I mean?"

Abby's brows drew down and she walked over to her daughter. Touching her lightly on the shoulders, she looked into Olivia's worried eyes. "I hope so, dear. Why?"

"Because Daddy's always asking if we are."

Concerned now, Abby pushed a wayward strand of Olivia's hair out of her eyes. "What do you tell him?"

"Well, I say yes, of course. But, he asks so often, I started to wonder, you know—" she shrugged and tears started to trickle down her face "—if we were."

Abby smiled before pulling her close for a hug. She understood the doubts that were running through her daughter's mind, doubts Jeff had planted. "Oh, honey," she whispered, kissing her daughter's forehead.

Olivia sniffed and swiped at her nose with the back of her hand. "You know, Mom, I think Daddy's unhappy."

"How do you know that?"

"A kid can always tell."

"But you're okay—right?"

"Right." Olivia forced a frail smile, winked and gave her mother a big squeeze before she ran off to her room to feed her pet rabbit and change into her party clothes.

Abby watched her daughter scurry up the stairs and then sat down on one of the dining room chairs. She knew her guests would arrive soon, but she needed a minute to compose herself and get her second wind. Inadvertently, Olivia had delivered a message that worried her.

She picked up a long-stemmed glass and gazed at the light playing on the crystal. Jeff's behavior had been strange recently. He'd become overbearing and protective. And then there was the matter of prying into her private life.

Shivering, she felt a premonition of doom. She'd known that Jeff was unhappy, and Olivia had just brought that point more directly into focus.

"So now what?" she asked herself.

Sighing, she realized there was nothing she could do. Not tonight, anyway. She set the glass back on the table and concentrated on the more important issue at hand: bringing J.R. and Gary and fifty thousand dollars together without causing World War III.

Chapter Five
A Dinner Party

Trying to knot his tie, Gary stalked around the bedroom. J.R. and Abby. What a combination! Even though Valene had grudgingly agreed to go to Abby's party, Gary wondered if he'd made the biggest mistake of his life by urging her to attend. Jerking at the tie, he swore and walked to the window. After opening the blinds, he looked over at Abby's house and frowned.

"Here, let me do that."

Turning, he saw Valene coming out of the bathroom. She was dressed only in her slip. Cream-colored lace and satin swished around her as she walked over to the bed and sat down, towelling dry her blond curls.

"Got it," he said, slipping the knot into place. "How do I look?"

Cocking her head, she grinned. "Like a million, give or take a few hundred thousand."

"J.R. should like that," he said cynically.

"Right. J.R. likes anything that has to do with money." She finished drying her hair and sighed. "I don't know why you insisted that we go to this party in the first place."

"I kinda got trapped into it," he admitted, sitting next to her on the bed.

"I thought so."

"It's just one night." He slipped his arm around her shoulders and kissed her cheek.

Her blue eyes darkened as she looked at him. "You can't know that for sure. He scares me," she admitted. "He ruined our lives once before."

"Yeah, well, that was a long time ago."

"Sometimes it seems like yesterday." She still remembered the pain of losing Lucy, her only child, and the lonely years between then and now.

"Come on, lighten up."

"I'll try," she said, standing and walking over to the closet. "I'll try." She shuffled through a few dresses and settled on a black and silver two-piece ensemble, slipping the top over her head.

When she struggled with the buttons, Gary smiled and walked over to her. "Here, let me get it," he said, nuzzling her neck as he fastened the dress. "Have I mentioned to you lately how much I love you?" he whispered, turning her so that he could look down into her worried face.

"Not in a while."

"Then maybe I should show you . . . ?"

"Now?"

"Now." He folded her into the strong circle

of his arms and pressed his lips to hers in a
kiss that was as passionate as it was desperate.
Valene was the one bright spot in his life, and
he'd almost lost her once before when he'd
been involved with another woman. He promised himself he'd never lose her again, even if it
meant taking on Abby, J.R., the Orchid Cab
Company and the rest of the world.

Carefully, so as not to hurt her, he lowered
her onto the bed.

Later, Val couldn't believe she'd let Gary talk her
into coming to the party. But here she was, in the
same house with J.R. As she stood in the dining
room, looking over the sumptuous dinner table,
she told herself to buck up. Even though she'd
had no intention of attending this affair, and
Karen and Gary had railroaded her into it, she
would just have to make the best of it.

She could hear the hum of conversation drifting from the living room: Karen's soft laughter,
J.R.'s steady Texan drawl, an occasional chuckle
from Sid, and the clink of ice cubes against
glass. Just the thought of being trapped in
Abby's house with J.R. made her skin crawl.

So why had she come? she asked herself
again. The answer was simple. She was here
because she loved Gary with all her heart and
she knew that she had to stand up to J.R. She
had to prove that their love could withstand
anything, even J.R. Ewing.

Taking a sip of wine, she walked to the edge
of the table and looked into the living room.
J.R. was leaning against the mantle, swirling a
mixed drink in one hand and smiling with self-

importance. The sight of him made Val's nerves tighten.

"Get a hold of yourself," she whispered to herself, taking another sip.

Sid wandered over to the table, took a look at the lavish spread and chuckled. Quiche, duck à l'orange, shrimp bisque, Waldorf salad, and a plate of fruits and cheeses graced the evening's menu.

Abby and Olivia were lighting the candles. Sid patted his sister on the shoulder. "I didn't know you could cook like this."

Olivia giggled. "She can't. She called a caterer."

Val smiled to herself. Of course. But why had Abby gone to all this trouble? She glanced at Gary as he entered the dining room, but he avoided her eyes.

A few minutes later, the guests had settled down around the table. Folding and refolding her napkin in her lap, Val waited. She knew that Abby had to have an ulterior motive for this party, and that whatever it was, it somehow involved Gary and J.R. Something was going on . . .

J.R. was seated directly across from her. He cleared his throat and raised his glass. "I'd like to toast our—"

Olivia squealed, reached across the table and slapped her brother. She was kicked in the shins for her efforts. "Ow! Brian!"

"What?" Brian asked, his face a picture of angelic innocence.

Val couldn't help but smile.

"You kicked me!" Olivia screamed.

"I did not!"

Karen attempted to break up the scene and shushed the children back into their places.

J.R. waited, obviously annoyed by the interruption, and then raised his glass again.

"I think it might be appro—"

"Ooohh!" Olivia shrieked at the top of her lungs and leaped from the table. A rubber lizard flew through the air. "Mommy! Brian's got that lizard again!" she said, pointing an accusing finger at her brother.

Gritting her teeth, Abby forced a smile at J.R. before motioning her daughter back to her place. "Calm down, Olivia. It hasn't bitten anybody yet."

"But, Mommy, he put it in my spinach!"

Abby's temper snapped. "Brian, that's enough!"

"I didn't do nothing—"

"*Any*thing. You didn't do anything," Karen cut in, trying to forestall a fight.

"See," said Brian.

J.R. leaned forward on his elbows, his cold eyes taking in each of Abby's kids. "Back home we know how to deal with unruly children," he said slowly, pausing for effect. "We barbecue 'em."

Olivia's eyes grew round, and Brian sat up straight in his chair. They looked to their mother for support, but she wouldn't say a word. Instead, her eyes were glued to J.R.

"As I was saying . . . a toast to family . . . and friends . . ." J.R. lifted his glass again and, standing, smiled down upon the group. Abby cheerfully raised her glass in acknowledgment.

Sid and Karen followed suit. But Val only went through the motions, barely touching her glass to Gary's.

Somehow she made it through the rest of the meal. As much as possible, she avoided J.R.'s stare and tried to comfort herself with the thought that the evening wouldn't last forever. She helped Abby clear the dishes, and by the time she returned to the living room, J.R. had cornered Sid.

"I was real impressed by your engine, Sid."

"Oh, thanks."

J.R. rubbed his hand over his chin. "One hundred miles per gallon! Ain't that something?"

"Well, I'm only getting about fifty-eight right now."

Karen walked up to her husband and linked her arm through his. She'd overheard part of the conversation and seen the gleam of interest in J.R.'s eyes; she knew she had to intervene. She'd learned to treat J.R. with the same respect she gave a rattlesnake: keep a safe distance and avoid riling him. Too bad Sid didn't do the same, she thought.

"We're trying some new alloys to see if the metal might make a difference. After we run some stress tests—"

"Is that when you'll get your patents?" J.R. asked.

"I just don't want to rush things. I'm still working on a radically new fuel injection system."

Karen realized that Sid had warmed to the subject and was about to give away the farm.

"How about some dessert?" she cut in, but Sid wasn't listening.

"It's all pretty exciting," he admitted, smiling eagerly. "You see, it works on the principle—"

Karen couldn't stand it any longer. "Sid, I don't think that J.R. is interested in all the fine details of your invention."

"Nonsense, Karen! I love to hear a creative mind at work," J.R. insisted.

Luckily, Sid caught the hint. "I do have a tendency to go on about it, I guess."

Relieved, she took his hand. "Come on, maybe we can help your sister in the kitchen. She said something about you helping out with after-dinner drinks."

Val hadn't had a chance to talk to Gary alone. Every time she'd tried to pull him aside, Abby or J.R or even Sid had stolen his attention. She started to walk up to him, but just as she did, Sid, toting a bottle of sherry, appeared from the kitchen and naturally stopped to talk with his favorite employee. Val dropped into the nearest chair.

Frustrated, she looked at J.R. He was standing at the window, staring out into the night. Dressed in an impeccably tailored charcoal-gray suit, expensive boots, and a crisp white shirt, he reeked of money.

Abby came into the living room and caught Valene watching J.R. with cold, assessing eyes. The tension in her body was palpable and seemed to radiate outward in waves of hostility aimed at J.R. Trying to head off the inevitable battle, Abby held out a silver tray filled with small cakes. "Val, have some dessert.

You hardly touched your meal."

"Thanks, Abby, but I'm really not hungry."

J.R. lifted his head, turned and sauntered up to his sister-in-law. Taking the chair next to hers, he leaned back and crossed his long legs. "You ought to eat when you're sitting at a full table, Valene . . . never can tell how long your good luck's going to hold."

"I'm not hungry!"

"I'm really sorry about that, Val," he mocked.

Refusing to be baited, she forced a grin and stood. "I guess it's not your problem, is it?"

Gary saw the storm brewing. Breaking away from Sid, he caught the tail end of the conversation and slipped his arm around his wife's shoulders.

Sid walked over to the bar, set the sherry on the shelf and, after checking the labels of the bottles, picked up a fifth of brandy. "Anyone for an after-dinner drink?"

"You can fill mine up," J.R. said. "Say, that deal Gary's working on ought to make you a dollar or two."

"What's that?" Sid asked, looking puzzled as he handed J.R. his glass.

"The deal Gary's working on."

"What deal?" Sid looked over to Gary. "What's he talkin' about?"

Valene felt Gary's arm stiffen around her shoulders and saw him pale. *Oh, God,* she thought. *So that's it; Gary's working on something behind Sid's back!* Her emotions churning, she turned accusing eyes on her husband and then finally on J.R. The tension among the three men charged through the air like an electric current.

J.R. caught himself and shook his head. "Now, isn't that funny? You know what I just did? I just confused my brother Gary with my brother Bobby. You ever do that sort of thing?"

Sid looked at him curiously, but J.R. didn't miss a beat. "You see, my brother *Bobby's* working on this project, and you were talking about Gary and for the life of me—I don't know why—I just locked into Bobby," he said smoothly.

"It's a sign of age, J.R." Sid said good-humoredly, but his eyes narrowed for a second on Gary.

Val felt Gary's fingers digging into her arms and realized how desperate he was. But why? What kind of a deal was he involved in? And how did J.R. know about it?

"Old age, is it? You must be right, Sid." J.R. smiled and then focused directly on Val, watching her reaction. "Say, Val, how about an after-dinner drink with your brother-in-law?"

"I don't think so." Biting back the urge to tell him off, she twisted away from Gary and walked out of the room. Not knowing where she was going, she stormed through the kitchen and out the back door.

The night air felt good against her face and cooled some of the anger burning deep inside. She walked across the lawn to the patio and closed her eyes until she stopped trembling. Then she sat down in a lounge chair and sighed.

"Why, Gary?" she wondered aloud as she

looked into the shimmering dark water of Abby's pool. "Why have you lied to me again?"

The Avery home was extremely quiet. Laura could hear the clock in the hall ticking and the steady hum of the refrigerator. As she sat at the kitchen table, trying to concentrate on her newest real estate listings, her mind continued to wander. Richard never felt much like going out anymore, and most of the time Laura was too tired to insist. So they had settled into a predictable routine, and the quiet, eerie tension between them mounted.

She took off her glasses, rubbed her eyes and looked up to see Richard staring out the window toward Abby's house. What a fool! If only he knew that she was using him, Laura thought miserably.

Richard held open the blinds and glared through the window. He was still furious that Abby had brushed him aside the other day. He hated her for treating him so badly, and yet, he still wanted her back in his life.

Pacing, he walked into the living room and then back to the kitchen to his post at the window. From his position he'd seen the guests arriving, recognized J.R. Ewing and known that something was happening—something big. Just now, Val had raced out of the house and slumped into a chair near Abby's pool. She had stared across the water before letting her face fall into her hands. Richard could only guess what had happened. And not knowing was driving him nuts. "What's going on over at Abby's?" he asked his wife.

"I don't know, honey." She looked up and offered him a kind smile.

Her sympathetic look bugged the hell out of him. "Looks like some big party." Richard craned his neck in an attempt to see who was involved. "Did Abby say anything to you about a dinner party?"

Laura shook her head and began rifling through the multiple listing book.

Feeling slighted, he threw back the curtain and marched over to the table. "You know, since you've been working, we hardly go anywhere anymore."

"Honey, that's not true."

"When was the last time we went out?" he asked.

Biting her lower lip, Laura thought for a moment and realized that she couldn't remember the last time she and Richard had been out together. Feeling guilty, she thought about her next night out—the evening she'd planned with David Souther.

Richard pointed an accusing finger into the opened book. "You get home from work and you're too tired to do anything. You barely get dinner on the table and then you collapse—"

"Honey . . ."

"I can't get a word out of you!" Richard ranted. He gestured wildly at the listing book and Laura's notes. "You're all involved in what you do all day long, and then when you come home, you have nothing to talk about!"

Seething now, Laura put aside her work and walked over to the stove. She poured herself a cup of coffee, and noticed that her hands were shaking. Trying to calm herself, she took a sip from her cup, leaned against the counter, and mentally counted to ten. Getting into another argument with Richard wouldn't solve anything. "I've tried to talk to you about the work I do, but you're never interested."

"That's because work isn't the only thing to talk about!" he shouted, and then pushed her paperwork off the table. The books and notes fluttered in the air and crashed to the floor.

"Richard!"

Leaning over the table, he gave her a killing look. "All work and no play makes Laura very boring. You're no fun anymore."

Laura gripped the handle of her cup until her knuckles turned white. "You're not exactly the life of the party yourself," she taunted, then met his angry glare with one of her own. "Okay, what would you like to do for fun, Richard?"

"We should go out more. See people. We're getting too isolated."

Ignoring the fact that a week's worth of work was strewn across the hardwood floor, Laura set her cup on the counter and crossed her arms over her chest. "What's the matter, Richard? Abby having a party and she didn't invite you?" Laura knew she was asking for a confrontation the minute the words left her mouth.

"That's not what I'm talking about!" he snapped.

"That *is* what you're talking about! Admit it!"

Trembling, Laura walked back to the table and began picking up her papers and books.

"Very cute, Laura. One of these days you're going to analyze yourself right out of this marriage."

Laura's anger exploded and she met Richard's furious gaze. "Is that a threat or a promise?"

"Guess." Richard wheeled around and returned to his silent vigil at the window. Knowing that his life was careening out of control, he felt helpless, scared and mad at the world. Especially at Laura. "Damn! Damn! Damn!" he muttered as he saw Val go back inside Abby's house.

To escape dealing with her brother-in-law, Val had offered to put Olivia and Brian to bed while Abby finished serving coffee. Now, pacing in the upstairs hallway, she tried to come up with an excuse to leave. Putting the kids to bed had worked, and she'd stretched it out as long as she could by reading them a couple of stories and asking them about school. But finally, she'd tucked them in, knowing she could not stay upstairs forever.

Hoping that Gary would catch the hint, Val glanced nervously at her watch as she walked down the stairs and stepped into the living room. It didn't work. Gary was too involved in a discussion with Karen, while J.R. and Sid were seated kitty-corner from each other on the L-shaped sofa. *Probably discussing that super-engine again*, she thought while wondering how to avoid her brother-in-law.

J.R. glanced at her and smiled—the same cold smile that made her insides quiver. "Yep," he said, agreeing with himself. "Our gal, Lucy, she's quite a handful!"

Val stopped dead in her tracks.

Karen looked up, saw the stricken expression on Val's face, and knew she had to do something to shut J.R. up.

"Lucy doesn't know the first thing about picking a man for herself. You ought to see the string of weirdos she's connected herself to— most peculiar brand of humans I've met this side of New York City," J.R. said, watching Val turn ashen. "I guess all things considered, this boy she's got her claws into now's about the best of a bad lot."

"What kind of work does he do?" Sid asked as Val walked slowly into the room.

"Medicine. But the dummy doesn't even have the sense to milk it for what it's worth. He's in research. Now how the hell he's gonna support Lucy's fancy tastes doing research is something that's gonna bear witnessing." J.R. shook his head and clucked his tongue.

"Maybe money's not important to them," Karen said.

J.R. shook his head and gave her a "you know better than that" look.

"A man can't have everything in life. He's got to make choices," Sid said, seeing the warning in Karen's eyes.

"Yeah, well, if these nuptials go through, I'm gonna help the boy make a few of them." J.R. said.

Vividly recalling how he had destroyed her life

and dominated Lucy, Val crossed the room and stood before the couch. "You're going to what?"

"Help him make some choices. Straighten him out. Don't you worry. Your daughter's a Ewing, Valene. We'll bring the boy up to our standards."

"I don't believe this," she said, glancing at Gary before turning her gaze back to J.R. "You just leave Lucy out of this!"

Gary, seeing his wife challenge J.R., held up his hand, silently pleading with her to leave well enough alone. "Honey—"

But Val wasn't finished. "How dare you meddle in my daughter's life, or that boy's life, or anybody's life, for that matter!"

J.R. seemed to stare right through her. "Lucy needs a strong hand to guide her. She hasn't had much mothering from you, after all—"

"How could she have? *You* wouldn't allow it."

"Miss Lucy seems pretty happy right where she is—"

"Would you even notice if she weren't happy?" Val was visibly shaking.

Gary came up to her and took her hand. "Hey, wait a minute, both of you. Come on, Valene. Calm down—"

"I will *not* calm down! He's the reason I never had my baby to raise on my own—that we've never had a proper family!"

"Is that so?" J.R. taunted, settling back on the cushions and eyeing Gary and Valene. How stupid they looked—Valene all hot with anger and Gary impotently trying to stop her from mouthing off.

Soaps & Serials™ Fans!

★ Order the *Soaps & Serials*™ books you have missed in this series.

★ Collect other *Soaps & Serials*™ series from their very beginnings.

★ Give *Soaps & Serials*™ series as gifts to other fans.

...see other side for ordering information

Soaps & Serials™
From Pioneer Communications
Network, Inc.

You can now order previous titles of *Soaps & Serials*™ Books by Mail!

Just complete the order form, detach, and send together with your check or money order payable to:

Soaps & Serials™
120 Brighton Road, Box 5201
Clifton, NJ 07015-5201

- - - - - - - - - - - - - - - - - -

Please circle the book #'s you wish to order:

(A) The Young and The Restless........	1	2	3	4	5	6	7	8	9	10
(B) Days of Our Lives....	1	2	3	4	5	6	7	8	9	10
(C) Guiding Light.......	1	2	3	4	5	6	7	8	9	10
(D) Another World......	1	2	3	4	5	6	7	8	9	10
(E) As The World Turns..	1	2	3	4	5	6	7	8	9	10
(F) Dallas™	1	2	3	4	5	6	7	8	9	10
(G) Knots Landing™.....	1	2	3	4	5	6	7	8	9	10

Each book is $2.50 ($3.50 in Canada).

Total number of books
circled_____ × price above = $ _____

Sales tax (CT and NY residents only) $ _____

Shipping and Handling $ _____ .95

Total payment enclosed $ _____
(check or money orders only)

Name _____

Address _____ Apt# _____

City _____

State _____ Zip _____

Telephone (_____) _____
Area Code

KL 10

"You know it's true!" Gary snapped.

J.R. looked to Sid and Karen and shrugged before turning back to the furious woman standing in front of him. "Now, Valene. I wouldn't want to be responsible for keeping you from your loved ones."

"Oh, no, of course you wouldn't," she said sarcastically. Tears were building in her eyes, and her chin, though trembling, jutted forward in defiance. "That's all you've ever done. That's all you've ever done to me. But you're not going to do it to Lucy!" She sputtered as she sought for more ammunition to launch at him, but the words wouldn't form. Spinning away from Gary's arms, she marched toward the door, nearly knocking over a table lamp in her fury.

Running out of the house, Val began to cry. She didn't care if she had ruined Abby's dinner party. The whole idea had been stupid and she'd been a fool to go along with it. All night long she'd listened to J.R. talking about cars and oil and brothers and deals, but she'd refused to sit still when he'd brought up the subject of Lucy. Dear, sweet Lucy.

With tears streaming down her cheeks, she kicked off her shoes, picked them up and raced toward the house that she and Gary had built. Why had J.R. come back to Knots Landing? And why, dear God, was Gary involved with him?

"Hey, what's going on?" Abby asked as she walked through the dining room and stared at the open door. "Was that Val?"

Gary didn't move. He was surprisingly calm as he stared down at his brother. "You bastard," he said. "You arrogant self-serving bastard." Then he strode out of the room and slammed the door behind him. The house was suddenly deathly quiet.

"What happened?" Abby demanded. Everything was ruined. All because of Gary's wimpy wife.

Karen was too stunned to speak. She'd just witnessed how J.R. could manipulate people and she felt guilty for insisting that Gary and Val join the party. It had been a mistake—a big mistake. And there was J.R., sitting on the couch as if none of the angry words had bothered him a bit.

He reached down for his cup of coffee, took a satisfied sip, and turned to Abby with a smile.

Karen felt sick. "I think we'd better go," she said, taking Sid's hand and urging him toward the door. The faster she could make tracks away from J.R. Ewing, the better.

As Val reached the front door and started fumbling with the lock, she was sobbing. "Oh, damn," she muttered as she dropped her key.

Gary caught up with her and grabbed her elbow. "Val—"

Still furious, she spun around and swiped at her tears. "Don't expect me to apologize!"

"I won't."

"I've lost the key, ruined my dress, all because of . . . all because of . . ."

"Shh." He touched the side of her face, catching a lingering tear before wrapping his arms around her. "It'll be all right. . . ."

"Oh, Gary, what's he doing here?" she said, clinging to him. "I mean, why's he here?"

"I don't know, Val. Some oil convention," Gary said, inwardly cringing at his lie.

"I don't mean that. What's he want from us?"

He let her go. "Oh, Val, for God's sake! It's just—"

"Gary, nothing's 'just' anything with your family. If he's here it's because he wants something!

He looked across the street to the lights in Abby's house. How could he explain to Val that he needed J.R., needed the Ewing money? What could he possibly say to wash away the hurt in her large eyes?

"You're not getting involved in any business deal with him, are you?"

"Of course not!" Gary said, ramming his fingers into his pockets and scowling into the dark night.

"It's not his style to show up for friendly family dinners."

"Stop being so suspicious. I said I wasn't involved with him. That's it!" He walked to the other side of the porch, and his boot scraped against metal; it was the key. Bending over, he picked it up, unlocked the door and walked into the hallway. Flipping on the lights, he stared at the comfortable home he'd made here in Knots Landing—away from J.R., away from the bottle, and away from the Ewing money. Now he was trapped all over again!

Val followed him inside. Swallowing back her

tears, she closed the door and leaned against it, but her eyes were trained on her husband and the tense lines near the corners of his mouth. "Gary, promise me you won't get involved with him, either."

"Valene—"

"He'll hurt you, Gary. Don't you know that by now?"

"I'm not involved with J.R.!" he said, closing his eyes.

"And you won't be . . . ?"

"No!"

Val wasn't going to rest until she was dead certain. "Promise me that!"

"I *promise*!" Gary yelled. Then, softly, almost resignedly, "I promise."

"Thank God." Val walked into the living room and pushed a lock of blond hair away from his eyes. Then she placed her palms on either side of his face and brushed a kiss over his lips.

Gary squeezed her, hating himself for his duplicity.

"It's just that sometimes I get so scared," she whispered. "I never want to go back."

"I know." He kissed the top of her head, smelled her perfume and silently cursed the fact that he had to lie to her.

But it was just a little lie, he told himself. One that she'd never uncover.

Chapter Six
Aftermath

Michael Fairgate was tossing darts at the wall when he heard the front door open and close. Knowing he'd be in big trouble if caught awake, he threw the dart board and darts into the closet, snapped off the light and jumped into bed, where he was supposed to have been hours ago.

The creak of the stairs warned him that his parents were headed for bed. Scrunching his eyes shut and facing the wall, he pretended to be asleep.

He heard the door open and noted light from the hall spilling into the room.

"Michael?" his mother whispered.

He didn't answer and hoped that his breathing looked regular. He felt Karen's lips brush against his cheek as she tucked his blankets under his chin.

When he heard the door shut, he let out a long sigh and tried to fall to sleep. But it was

impossible. He tossed and turned on the bed.
The sheets bunched around his legs, and he
couldn't keep his eyes closed for anything.

Maybe his mother could help. She always
knew how to calm him down. Reluctantly
Michael snuck out of his room and headed for
his parents' bedroom. Once there, he stopped
and listened to the conversation sifting through
the door.

In the bedroom, Sid was staring through the
window. He could see Abby's house and the
ridiculous silver limousine parked at the front
curb. So J.R. was still inside with Abby. What
were they cooking up? He shifted from one leg
to the other and told himself it didn't matter.
Abby could take care of herself; she didn't need
an older brother poking his nose into her life.

Karen changed into her nightgown and
slipped into bed. Sid didn't even notice; he was
too absorbed in his thoughts. She propped up
the pillows and leaned back, her dark hair
fanned against the white sheets.

"Isn't he ever going to leave?" he muttered
as he walked toward the bed.

"They're probably having a nightcap, Sid.
Abby's a big girl, as you're so fond of pointing
out." She pushed back the covers and patted
the mattress. "Come on."

He slipped off his clothes, tossed them over
the bureau, and slid between the cool sheets.

"Isn't that better?" she asked, wrapping her
arms around him and placing her head on his
chest. She could hear the steady beating of his
heart. It was a comforting sound after all the
bitterness and pain she'd seen at Abby's party.

Sid still seemed lost in thought. He held her, but Karen felt that he was miles away.

"Remember me?" she asked, kissing his chest.

"How could I forget?" He kissed the top of her head and hugged her close. "You looked in on Michael. How was he?"

"He was asleep," Karen said, stretching lazily against him.

"He seems to be sleeping through the night again. That's good."

"Is it?" she asked, propping up on one elbow and looking her husband straight in the eye. "Does he seem better to you?"

"Uh-huh."

"How?"

"He's calmer. We must be doing something right."

"I don't know. I'm still worried," Karen admitted, looking up at the ceiling.

"I don't think that worrying does him any good. I think that was part of the problem in the first place. Too much pressure on the guy."

"Too much pressure? What do you mean? You know the doctor said we had to do everything we could to give him special attention."

Sid yawned. "Just to let him know we love him . . ."

"But more than that, Sid. I'm not talking about putting more pressure on him, I'm talking about giving him what he needs." She sat up and looked at him incredulously.

"And I think you have a tendency to coddle him too much."

"Coddle him?" she repeated, climbing out of

the bed and pacing the floor. "Coddle him?"

"Yes. You're acting like he's some sort of freak and he isn't!"

"I'm not treating him like a freak, I'm treating him like a boy, *my son*, who's in trouble, and who needs my help," Karen said.

"I don't think we're helping him by bending over backward and making him feel there's something wrong with him," Sid said.

"But there *is* something wrong with him, Sid. . . . I thought you finally understood that."

"I do understand. He's got a condition and it's being treated. Let's not overdo it." With a sigh, Sid rolled over and tried to go to sleep.

Karen got back into the bed, snapped off the lights, and thought about her youngest boy. Why was everything going wrong at once, not only at home but with the neighbors? Jeff and Abby, Val and Gary, Richard and Laura, and Kenny and Ginger. It seemed as if everyone she knew was going through a crisis. And what about her own family? Sid was wrapped up in his damned super-car, Diana was acting like a spoiled brat, Eric was gone more than he was home. And Michael. Dear, sweet, unhappy Michael, trying so hard in a world that didn't understand him.

A freak? They think I'm a freak! Outside the closed door, Michael swallowed and refused to let out the sob burning in his chest. He reached forward, touched the doorknob, and then let his hand drop. With a feeling of despair, he turned toward his room. *I'm not a freak*, he told himself as he tumbled into his bed, but he couldn't stop the tears that drizzled down the sides of his head and dampened his pillow.

Having cleared out the guests earlier than planned, Abby tried to make the best of a bad situation. She stood at her bar, looked over the half-empty bottles, and offered J.R. another drink.

"Don't mind if I do," he said.

She refilled his glass, then returned to the couch and sat down next to him.

The scene with Val had left Abby somewhat at a loss for words. What a self-righteous idiot that woman could be! All on her own, Val had probably ruined Gary's chances of getting money out of his brother. Abby knew that the prospects of arranging the fifty thousand dollar loan were now teetering between slim and none. But she was ready to play out the hand and see what she could still ante up to stay in the game with J.R. So she sipped her sherry, crossed her legs and met his interested gaze.

"You are about the most delicious conniver I've ever had the pleasure of encountering," he said.

"I beg your pardon?"

He stared into his drink before meeting her eyes. "My sister-in-law never had the vaguest notion of moving back to Dallas."

"I guess I was wrong," she said, a faint smile playing on her full lips.

"I guess you were," laughed J.R. "And I guess that about knocks hell out of any reason to give my brother fifty thousand dollars."

"I'm sorry to hear that," she replied, her voice low and husky. She coiled her body

seductively and let her lower lip protrude in a
beautiful pout; her wide blue eyes gleamed
with determination.

"You're a tough little fighter," he admitted,
watching her toss her golden hair away from
her face. "I like that. It's a shame that my
brother's not married to somebody like you
instead of the wimp he's been calling a wife. I
wouldn't mind having you in my family.
You're somebody I can talk to—even if you do
deal in 'stolen parts.'"

"Who said they were stolen?" Abby
demanded, her eyes narrowing.

He glanced over at her and convinced her
with a knowing glance that he wasn't a total
idiot. "And I've just got a feeling that somebody wants that fifty grand or my little brother's kneecaps, real bad. All of which puts Gary
in a terrible bind . . . having to choose between
me and not walking for the rest of his life."

"You're a very astute man."

"And you're a sharp lady. We understand
each other, you and me. I sure would like it if
we had more women like you in Texas."

"I sure would like it if you'd reconsider the
loan. It's important to Sid. He's my brother,
and I want to help him." She circled the top of
her glass with her finger, but stared at J.R.

"Honey, Sid doesn't even know that deal's
going through."

"Don't call me 'honey'!"

"Now, now. Don't get yourself all heated up,
honey." He paused for effect and let his eyes
slide slowly up Abby's body.

She shifted, trying to appear angry, but letting the hem of her dress slide upward over her thigh.

J.R. touched her knee. "Don't worry, honey. I'll give it to him. I'll give it to him . . . if and when he asks me for it." He set his drink down and circled her shoulder with one arm while running his fingers along the hem of her dress, pushing it upward, exposing more of her leg, feeling the softness of her skin through her thin stocking. "Of course, there is something I'll be wanting in return . . . from you."

"I thought so . . ." Abby said, her heartbeat fluttering, her breath shallow.

J.R. pulled her closer while his finger continued its deliberate climb to the top of her thigh.

Abby felt a wave of desire wash over her; there was something luring her closer to this powerful man. But she had to keep a cool head and remember what it was she was really after: the money.

As he leaned closer, his mouth brushing her cheek, Abby pressed a finger to his lips.

"Let's take care of business first," she suggested.

"I am, honey," he whispered. Pushing aside her finger, he claimed her mouth with his. She felt the power of his body pressing against hers, the warmth of his hands—one pushing the small of her back closer, the other caressing her hair.

She had to force herself to push him away. "Business first," she repeated, her lips warm, her breathing altered.

He looked at her and straightened his shirt. Standing, he shrugged into his coat and smiled.

"You know, it took me awhile to figure out what your interest was in this deal . . . what you wanted out of me."

"I don't want a thing for myself."

Laughing, J.R. placed his hat on his head and adjusted the brim. "Oh, yes you do, honey." Pausing to run his eyes over her one more time, he nodded to himself. "You want Gary."

The next morning Abby's spirits were soaring as she drove to work. She felt good about life. The sky was clear and blue, and the air smelled faintly of the sea as it blew in from the open window.

But best of all, she'd made a deal with J.R.!

She snapped on the radio and hummed along with the current pop tune. Taking the curves of the highway with a little more speed and recklessness than usual, Abby grinned.

As disastrous as the evening before had seemed to be when Gary had chased after Valene, Abby had managed to pull off her plans and secure a line of credit for him. All he had to do was ask his big brother.

Getting him to appeal to J.R. was going to be her final job, she decided, and not an easy one at that.

Pulling into the parking lot, she let the car idle and waited for Gary. When she saw his pickup turn into the lot, she turned off the engine and watched as he strode over to her. She couldn't help but smile when he opened her door to help her out.

"'Morning," he said as they walked briskly toward the building. The sun was warm against

Abby's back and a slight breeze moved the clouds in the hazy blue sky. "You really put me in a spot last night. What are you up to?"

Abby smiled brilliantly at him and winked as she unlocked the door. "I'm 'up to' fifty thousand dollars . . . the fifty thousand that you'll be needing in a few days. I can get it from your brother."

Gary crossed his arms over his chest. "I'll get it my own way."

"How? Is Chicken Little going to drop it out of the sky on you? You can't go to a bank. You won't ask anybody else in your family . . ."

"I can't take money from J.R."

Abby brushed past him and hurried inside the building. "Why? Because Valene hates him? Gary, you're going to get hurt if you don't get hold of that money. And I don't want you to get hurt." She turned to face him, her eyes filled with concern. She wanted to make things easy for him and wished that he would just give up and listen to her. Reaching forward, she gently touched his sleeve, but he jerked away from her.

"Abby, there's been such a lot of trouble between me and J.R. over the years."

"What's that got to do with his giving you a simple loan of fifty thousand dollars?"

The lines around Gary's mouth deepened. "You don't know my brother. It's not a simple loan. It's business. And doing business with J.R. . . ."

". . . will keep you out of a wheelchair. Get smart. It's the only way, and you better recognize that before it's too late."

Disgusted, Abby spun around and stalked

into her office, leaving Gary to deal with the
demons in his mind. Sooner or later he'd have
to face facts. She slammed the door and sat
down at her desk, still furious with him for not
listening to reason.

The sun hung low in the sky, filtering through
the leaves of the tree in Karen's back yard and
dappling the garden with shadowed light. The
scent of summer flowers filled the air and
insects droned as Jeff and Karen walked into
the kitchen.

"Stick around—have a cup of coffee," Karen
suggested. She'd spent over an hour talking
with him and hated to see him leave. Jeff sat at
the kitchen table and accepted a cup. Cradling
it in his hands, he stared into the black liquid.

"Okay," Karen said, taking the seat opposite
his. "You've told me about your past with
Abby and the kids, and you even touched upon
your job. But what about the future?"

"I don't know," he admitted, shaking his
head. "I just don't know."

The sound of the garage door cranking open
announced Sid's arrival. A minute later he
walked through the back door. "Hi, honey . . .
Jeff." He leaned over the table and kissed
Karen's cheek before turning to Jeff. "Staying
for dinner?"

Jeff checked his watch and shook his head.
"No thanks, Sid. I just stopped by for a cup of
coffee and to talk to Karen for a while." He
smiled at them and rose. "Thanks . . . for
everything."

Karen shrugged easily. "Anytime." She followed Jeff to the front door. When she returned to the kitchen, she found Sid at the table with a cup of his own and the evening paper.

"More problems?" he asked, looking over the top of the business section.

"The same ones."

Frowning, he snapped his paper. "I'd appreciate it if you didn't discuss them."

"Why?"

"Abby's my sister. I don't feel comfortable having her life dissected at my dinner table."

"She may be your sister, and this may be uncomfortable, but unfortunately her life is affecting lots of other people."

"Let's not get started."

"It's been going on from the day Abby pulled into the cul-de-sac!" She rummaged through the pantry, located a kettle, then slammed it onto the stove.

"Karen, I really don't want to talk about this." Ignoring his paper and the argument he saw brewing, Sid scraped his chair back and started to walk out of the room.

Karen was right on his heels. "I understand your loyalty to Abby. I respect it. But what about some loyalty for the rest of your family? For your friends? This is a small neighborhood, and your sister is a *big* problem."

"What does that mean? A *big* problem."

"I'll tell you. She borrows things and they disappear. She asks for favors but never returns even one. She's been sleeping with the husband of one of our best friends—an affair that everyone, including your kids and your niece and nephew, knows about. She can't seem to

find the time to care for her children, so Val's
become their surrogate mother. And ever since
she's been working for you, something's been
happening between her and Gary. I don't
know what, but something, I'm sure of it."

"You always are." He started up the stairs.

"Where Abby's concerned, you're right.
She's your baby sister and I know what that
means to you, but she's trouble and I don't
know any other way to say it. The sooner you
take off your blinders, the better for all of us—
you, me, our children, our friends, everyone—
including Abby."

She followed him into the bedroom and
watched as he unbuttoned his shirt. When he
looked at her, she stared pointedly into his eyes
and waited for a reaction.

Anger and pain flashed in his face, but still
he refused to fight. Instead, he ripped off his
shirt, threw it onto the bed, and then sat down
to pull off his shoes.

Furious, she turned and hurried out of the
bedroom, leaving Sid to sort out the truth and
reach his own conclusions.

Karen raced down the stairs and swept into
the kitchen. Once at the counter, she leaned
against the edge and took several deep breaths.
Looking out the window, she noticed that the
sun was about to set. Though it was still warm,
a chill slid down her spine. She had the sudden, undeniable feeling that a major calamity
was about to ruin her life.

Chapter Seven
Confrontations

"Another day, another dollar," Abby told herself with a sigh as she poked through her closet looking for something to wear. The morning sunshine filtered through her open window, rustling the loose weave of her curtains and brightening her room, but she barely noticed.

She was growing weary of her battle with the Ewings. First with J.R., and now with Gary. Why couldn't it all be less complicated? "If only Gary wasn't so darn stubborn, all his problems would be solved," she muttered as she jerked a white sun dress off its hanger.

She tossed the garment on the unmade bed and then stripped out of her silk nightgown. Trying to raise her flagging spirits, she slid into the dress and shook out her curls while trying to come up with a scheme to force the Ewing brothers together.

"We're leaving, Mom," Olivia called from downstairs.

"Have a good day," Abby said. She glanced out the window to see Olivia and Brian dash across the front yard toward the bus stop at the corner. "And you have a good one, too," she told herself as she caught her reflection in the oval mirror over the bureau. "At least try!"

She finished dressing, threw the bed together, went downstairs and scowled at the messy kitchen table. Two boxes of cereal were sitting next to an opened container of milk. Bits of sugar-coated cereal floated in the bottom of two bowls, and Brian's forgotten homework had a big stain on it.

"Wonderful," she said, putting the milk away, then pouring a cup of coffee. "This is starting out as another great day in the life of Abby Cunningham!"

After a few quick swallows, she dashed the remains of her coffee into the sink, rinsed out the cup, ignored the mess on the table and walked through the house to the front door.

She was still on the front porch when she noticed an unfamiliar car parked near the curb. A clean-cut young man climbed out of the battered auto and walked up the flagstone steps toward her.

"Mrs. Abby Cunningham?" he asked, his dark eyes looking directly into hers.

Abby smiled warmly. "Hi."

He crossed the few steps between them, pulled an envelope from his back pocket, and handed it to her.

"What the devil?" she said, watching as he quickly spun around and started to walk back to his beat-up Chevy. "Hey, wait—" But he was almost to the car. Frowning, she quickly tore open the envelope and began to read. "Order to Show Cause? Custody hearing? Wait, young man, come back here! What is this?"

He called over his shoulder, "I don't write them, ma'am. I just deliver them. Sorry . . ."

He climbed into his car and sped off. Abby stared after the blue plume of smoke billowing in his wake. Then, not really believing that she'd actually been served custody papers, she frantically reread the document again and again.

"That bastard!" she hissed, thinking about Jeff while her fury finally consumed her. Wadding the notice into a ball, she clenched it in her tiny fist. "You can't do this to me! I won't let you!" she said, storming back into the house and flopping down on the sofa. The kids. Oh, God, she did not want to lose the kids. . . .

Desperate, she realized she needed help. But from whom? She looked out the window to her brother's house. Sid. He would help her; he'd helped her ever since they were kids. When she'd been down and out, he'd even given her a job.

He'd help her now. He had to. She didn't have anywhere else to turn.

The clutter of morning breakfast dishes, bits of the newspaper, and uneaten toast and jam covered Karen's kitchen table. But she didn't care. Lounging in her robe, she leaned back in her chair and sipped coffee with Sid.

Neither one of them had mentioned their argument of the night before and Karen wasn't about to start in again. The morning was too perfect. She'd opened the French doors to the garden and the scent of roses filled the room. Diana, Eric and Michael had rushed off to school without any major battles, and Karen was enjoying the peace and quiet of being in the house alone with Sid.

The doorbell chimed, and then someone began beating furiously on the door. "Hold on, I'm coming," Karen said, tying the belt of her robe more tightly around her waist.

"Want me to get it?" Sid asked, starting to stand.

"Stay put." Karen smiled and waved him back into his chair. "Read your paper. One of the kids probably forgot something."

By the time she reached the door, the bell rang again. "Just a minute—" When she started to open the door, Abby burst in.

Blowing by Karen into the entry way, Abby looked into the living room. "I need to talk to Sid," she said.

"What's wrong, Abby? You look like you've seen a ghost."

"Is Sid still here?"

"In the kitchen." Before Karen could say anything else, Abby raced down the hallway.

Sid was still seated at the breakfast table.

"Thank God you're here," she whispered. She placed the crumpled court order on the table in front of him.

"What's going on?"

"Jeff's suing me for custody of the children!"

"What?" Sid adjusted his reading glasses before he smoothed the paper and attempted to read the notice.

Karen felt cold inside. She walked over to the table and read the document over his shoulder. "He didn't say anything about going to court," she whispered, guilt twisting her insides.

"No, he didn't have to, once he got the information he wanted," Abby shot back, her furious blue eyes narrowing at her sister-in-law.

Sid pinched the bridge of his nose, removed his glasses and tried to put the messy situation into perspective. Shaking his head, he looked up at Abby, scowling. "You're going to need a lawyer."

"I want the best there is, Sid. Someone who'll cut Jeff to shreds and stop him dead!"

"Michael Maddox. He's a customer," Sid said.

Karen, still in shock, sat down at the table and pushed her dark hair from her eyes. "Do you really think Jeff is serious about this?"

Sid waved the paper under Karen's nose. "This looks pretty serious to me."

Abby was beside herself with rage. Her cheeks were flushed and she was shaking. "God, I hate Jeff for doing this! And I hate having to play his stupid game—"

"You don't have much choice right now. And Maddox knows all the rules. He'll be a good man to have in our corner. I'll get his number." Sid sighed, pushed back his chair and started to walk into his den.

"You'll come with me, won't you?"

"Where? To meet with Maddox?"

Abby nodded. "Please."

Sensing her uncertainty and fear, Sid placed his arm around her shoulders and gave her a hug. "Right away."

Holding him tightly, she whispered, "Thanks."

"No problem." He looked over Abby's shoulder and his angry eyes met Karen's.

She was still stunned. Shaking her head, she met Sid's accusing stare and silently mouthed the words, "I didn't know."

"Okay. Buck up," he said to Abby. "I'll call Maddox right now."

While Abby paced the floor, Sid went into the den, dug up Maddox's number and gave him a call. A few minutes and two secretaries later, he was connected with Maddox and filled him in on the details of Abby's situation. "She's pretty upset, Mike. Any way we can see you today?"

Maddox talked to his secretary and rearranged his schedule. "Have her come downtown in an hour," he suggested.

"Thanks." Relieved, Sid hung up the phone and walked back into the kitchen. "We lucked out," he told Abby. "Maddox will see us in an hour."

"Thank God," Abby murmured, shooting Karen an angry glare that said more clearly than words, "this is all your fault!"

Karen sat in the kitchen and sipped her coffee while Sid and Abby discussed different ways of fighting Jeff. She remembered the sad look on Jeff's face as he'd sat in their kitchen the night before. She'd known then something was bothering him that he just couldn't bring himself to talk about.

Now she wished she could have said the right words or done something to prevent the bloody battle that was brewing. Poor Olivia and Brian—caught in the middle.

She stared out the window and heard Abby and Sid leave. She thought back to the day she'd admitted to Jeff that Abby was having an affair with Richard. Shivering, she realized just how ugly the whole situation could get. Her testimony could drive a wedge between herself and her husband and Abby.

There were no winners in custody battles, and now the losers would be surrounding her and blaming her for her part in the mess.

Abby and Sid got into his car without a word. As Sid drove down the quiet cul-de-sac and onto the main road, Abby rolled down her window, letting the cool morning breeze filter in. She felt trapped, snared, caught struggling for her life. All because of Jeff—and Karen! Leaning back in the seat, she tried to calm down and concentrate on the wind blowing her blond hair and cooling her flushed cheeks.

"Don't worry," Sid said, patting her arm. "Maddox will straighten this out." But he didn't meet her eyes. Instead he concentrated on the curving road and traffic, his hands tense on the wheel, his brow grooved with deep lines.

He parked the car across the street from the concrete and glass high-rise complex housing the law offices of James, Smith, McKenna and Maddox.

The street was jammed with people. There were vendors hawking exotic foods and drinks. Mimes roamed up and down a brick amphitheater nearby, putting on a show for the crowd. Musicians had set up their own little stages in various corners of the mall next to the skyscraper.

Sid took hold of Abby's elbow and urged her up the steps and into the courtyard of the main building. A large fountain sprayed upward into the hazy sky, and people clustered around the shimmering blue pool of water.

The area was bursting with life, yet Abby walked absently through the revolving glass doors of the building, feeling numb. Completely wrapped up in her own world, she could think only about the kids and how empty her life would be without them.

Once inside the law office on the sixth floor, Abby and Sid were ushered into a large corner suite with floor-to-ceiling windows and a panoramic view of the ocean. Abby shook the hand of a short, slightly balding man in his midforties, and then dropped into one of the leather chairs in front of his desk.

Mike Maddox motioned Sid into the chair next to Abby's, settled back in his own, then crossed his arms over his chest. "Okay, Mrs. Cunningham. I'm going to spell it out for you. Custody hearings usually start out nasty, cruel, and humiliating. From there it's generally downhill."

As Sid and Abby exchanged glances, Mike stood and started to pace around the office. "Why? Because it's a *legal* proceeding that tries to make a moral evaluation.'' Stopping at Abby's chair, he stared pointedly at her. ''A moral evaluation of you.''

''Why me? What about Jeff?'' she gasped, her cheeks coloring.

Mike smiled coldly. ''How many men have you slept with since your divorce, Abby? One, two, ten, twenty?''

Stunned, Abby shot Sid a worried look before training her eyes on the man in front of her. ''What?''

''Got a boyfriend? Who is he? What's he do? How often does he come to the house? Does he spend the night? Where are the children?''

''I don't have a boyfriend!''

''Oh, I see. You prefer to play the field. A swinger.''

''*What!*''

His eyes darkening, Sid held up his hand. ''Mike—''

''Hold on, Sid,'' Mike ordered before turning back to Abby. ''Ever smoke grass? Snorted coke? Gone to a porno movie?''

Abby was so furious, she was shaking. She met the attorney's gaze and gripped the arms of her chair until her hands ached. ''What are you trying to do?''

He smiled and shrugged. ''Give you a little taste of what you can expect. That's all.''

''That's ridiculous!''

''Not at all. Jeff's lawyer has got to prove you're an incompetent mother. You're not a criminal or a drug addict or a child abuser, right? So he's got to attack your morals. And attack means *attack* !''

"Well, I'm not losing my children! What can I do to defend myself?"

Mike's bland face softened with sincerity. "The surest way is for you and your husband to iron out your problems before you get to court."

"That's impossible!"

"Why?"

"We're beyond reasoning. Look, he doesn't really want custody. He's using this to force me to live the way he wants me to live," she admitted, her shoulders slumping a little.

"That's not unusual."

Sid tapped his fingers on the edge of the chair. "Still . . . you can't prove that, can you?"

"No," Mike said, returning to his chair.

"So let's go to court," Abby suggested.

"I'd try to avoid that if I were you," he said, rubbing his chin.

Sid was confused. "Why? I thought the courts still favored the mothers?"

"More often than not, but there are too many variables: judgmental judges and, frankly, times are changing. Fathers win more of these cases every day. Tell me, what's he like—your ex-husband?"

"He's a jerk!" Abby said, her chin jutting forward defiantly.

"Is that how he comes across? As a jerk? A nut? Eccentric?"

Sid rubbed his chin. "Not really. He can be impressive. He comes across as sincere, intelligent, affectionate—a good man."

"He's all hype!" Abby said bitterly.

Tenting his hands together, Mike offered an encouraging smile. "Look, give it a try, Abby. Swallow your pride. Clean up your act, if your act's a little dusty. See Jeff, try to iron out your differences. It'll be a small price to pay to avoid the risk of losing your children."

Abby pursed her lips but sat in silence and tried to weigh the facts. Placing her head into her palm she mentally cursed her situation. It was so bloody unfair! She steadied herself and decided she was not going to be a victim in this battle. She knew this was one fight she was going to win. Standing, she offered her hand to the attorney. "Thank you for your time, Mr. Maddox. I'll take your advice. But if it doesn't work, I'll be back."

"It'll work," he said, shaking her small hand. "If you want it badly enough."

"Oh, I do," she said, her eyes gleaming with determination. "I do."

When Laura Avery came downstairs for breakfast, the kitchen seemed unusually dark and gloomy. Telling herself she was imagining things, she walked over to the blinds, drew them up and flung open the windows. Brilliant morning sunlight, the merry chirping of birds, and the sweet scent of blooming oleander filled the room, but they still didn't help her bad mood.

It was probably all because of Richard, she thought.

Seated at the table, still in his pajamas, Richard was reading the morning newspaper and sipping a cup of coffee. He seemed oblivious to her entrance.

"Good morning," she said, forcing a smile.

Richard scarcely looked up. "'Morning," he grumbled.

"Beautiful day, isn't it?"

"Hadn't noticed."

Laura decided to forget breakfast and go straight to the office. She was already dressed, and nothing was preventing her from walking out the door—except for a sense of guilt about Richard. The fact that she was his wife and should at least make breakfast or coffee for him gnawed at her.

Liberated, I'm not, she thought, glancing out the window again. "I've got a business dinner tonight. I'll probably be late."

Richard finally looked up from his paper. His expression was one of total boredom. "Ah, yes," he mocked. "The crushing schedule of the woman on the way up. You ought to be single, Laura, with a condo at the beach, a 450 SL and—"

Laura's temper shot sky-high. "Damn it, Richard! You ought to be happy I've got a job!"

"Job! Your career has become an obsession!"

"Maybe it has, but I don't care! I'm tired of this, tired of *you*! If you're not moping around the house resenting my success, you're acting like a fool with our next-door neighbor."

Richard snapped his mouth shut and glared at her.

Laura couldn't stop. "I come home and if you've gotten home before me, you're in a black funk, and Jason's eaten another TV dinner and gone to bed in his school clothes. If I try to talk to you, you tell me to leave you alone. When I'm working, you're angry that I'm not here. So tell me, Richard! What do you want? What?''

Wearing a pained expression, Richard stared silently at his wife. Then he placed his hands on the table, stood up, and walked deliberately from the kitchen.

Laura felt her insides crumbling as she watched him leave. *Fight back, Richard*, she thought. *Fight back and show me you still have some pride left, that you still care!* But he'd slunk back into his dark hole instead. She heard the bottles clinking in the living room, knew that he was already fixing himself a drink. After waiting for several minutes, she tucked her purse under her arm, grabbed the listing book and walked out of the house.

When Richard finally heard Abby's car drive in that evening, he waited a respectable amount of time and then headed over to see what he could stir up with her.

Knocking softly, he entered the kitchen and found Abby busily preparing what appeared to be an elaborate dinner. Pots and pans were strewn all over the kitchen, vegetable peelings and shavings were piled in the sink, and, several empty boxes were splayed across the counter.

''What's going on?'' he asked.

''Nothing,'' Abby snapped, looking for her old cookbook—the one she'd used while she'd been married to Jeff.

''Expecting company *again*?'' he asked.

Irritated, she looked up at him. "Right. I'm expecting company. Again."

"Anyone I know?" He slouched into one of the chairs and stared at the mess in the kitchen.

"Jeff."

"Jeff?" he repeated, "Jeezus, Abby, *why*?"

She took a deep breath, found the book, dusted it off and started flipping through the pages.

"Well?"

She looked up sharply. "He's suing me for custody of the kids! That's why."

"Holy mother of—"

"That's not exactly what I said," she muttered, cutting him off. "I had to practically beg him to come over here." Still galled, she remembered the humiliating conversation with Jeff, how she'd pleaded with him to come and visit her to try and work things out peacefully. She slammed the cookbook closed.

"But why? What's he want them for?"

Exasperated, Abby rummaged around until she found her purse, pulled out the legal document and tossed it onto the table.

Richard scanned the pages quickly. "He's serious about this, isn't he?"

"Apparently." She turned back to the cookbook.

"But why?"

Deciding it would shut him up, Abby unloaded the whole story about the custody suit, starting with the day Jeff had found her on the chaise by the pool with him—her neighbor's husband.

Richard rubbed his stubbled chin, leaned back

in his chair and thought for a minute. "At least we know where we stand. We'll sit down, think this thing through—"

"I've already got a lawyer, Richard."

Feeling as if he'd just been slapped, he stared at her for a moment. Still stunned, he asked, "Who?"

"A man Sid recommended."

"I could handle this, Abby. Why did you ask Sid?" he asked quietly, his eyes boring into hers.

"Because I don't want you involved! My lover as my lawyer? That'll sound great at the hearing."

"I see," he said, as if he really didn't.

"I'm fighting for my kids and I won't give Jeff anything to work with. *Nothing!*"

Standing, Richard began to pace between the window and the table. "All right. Then I'll coach you on how to testify."

Carrying a kettle of boiling water from the stove to the sink, she waved him out of her way. "We can't be together, Richard," she said after putting the kettle on the tile counter and pushing a sweaty lock of hair from her eyes.

"Wait a minute, what do you mean? All this could take months. We'll never see each other."

"I'm talking about my children, for God's sake!"

"Abby, you're overreacting." He walked over and tried to touch her shoulder, but she shifted away from him.

"Maybe. But better to be overcautious than take this kind of risk."

Watching her, he let out a long, weary sigh. "Abby, I need you," he pleaded.

"But I don't need you, Richard," she said through clenched teeth. When she saw the color drain from his face, she softened somewhat. "You know that I like you and I enjoy you, but I don't need you. I've got my kids, my job, a whole new life ahead of me." She paused to shuffle two pots on the stove and tried to avoid the stricken look in his eyes. "An affair with the next-door neighbor . . . a married man . . ." Shaking her head, she looked into the oven and checked the timer. "Look, you're going to have to excuse me."

"Abby—"

"Richard, please. Just leave."

Squaring his shoulders, he cleared his throat. "Yeah, okay, sure."

She bit her lower lip and touched him on the shoulder. "Listen, it was nice. All of it. Let's hang on to that, okay?"

Angered by the way she could file him away like an old memo, Richard jerked away from her. "No. I'm not big on faded memories. And I'm a rotten loser." He threw open the door and walked briskly outside.

Abby watched him leave, feeling a twinge of remorse. "Forget him," she told herself. "You've got enough problems as it is." Closing the door, she turned her attention back to the meal she was preparing. "One step at a time. First you've got to convince Jeff that the kids are better off here. And then there's still Gary and J.R. Ewing. Abby, you've got your work cut out for you!"

Chapter Eight
First Kiss . . . Last Kiss

Abby put her hand to her brow and frowned at the mess in her kitchen. Every cooking utensil she had was dirty, the counters were barely visible, bowls and pots filled the sink. "Jeff had better fall for this," she muttered, thinking that cooking was for the birds. "Between being served with those lousy papers, seeing that obnoxious little attorney and having to give Richard the heave-ho, it's been one helluva day already."

Wiping her hands on a dishtowel, she looked longingly out the back window to the pool. What she needed was a break, but she didn't have time to sun-bathe. Good Lord, she hadn't even made dessert.

Hearing the mail arrive, she walked out the front door to get it. Glancing across the street to the Ewings' house, she scowled. Val was probably still stewing about the blow-up with J.R. at the party. "The woman has no backbone at all," she told herself as she grabbed her mail and sorted through the assortment of bills and advertisements. Then, stuffing the envelopes into her pockets, she decided to take the bull by the horns. Having Val mad at her would only make things worse. Right now she needed all the friends she could get.

She dashed across the street and knocked on the front door. Val opened it a second later.

"Hi . . . I, uh, thought I should explain about last night," Abby said.

"Explain what?" Val asked, not moving out of the doorway. Her lips were pressed firmly together and her eyes were ice-cold.

"About J.R."

"There's nothing to say. J.R.'s J.R."

"I know." Abby shrugged her shoulders. "But I did set up the party."

"Why? What did you get out of it?"

"Nothing! Look, I just met J.R. downtown and thought it would be nice if the two brothers could get together. That's all."

"You just *met* him?" Val asked and then waved her hand as if it didn't matter. "Forget it. What's done is done. There's no love lost between J.R. and me, and it's over. Okay?"

"You're sure?" Abby asked, offering a tentative smile.

"Yeah. Come on in, have a glass of iced tea." She stepped away from the door and Abby entered the cozy little house.

"I guess I shouldn't have meddled," she said. "But then I'm not really thinking straight nowadays."

"Oh?" Val headed into the kitchen and

Abby followed. "What's the problem?"

"It's Jeff. He's got me so crazy with this custody suit!"

"Custody suit?" Val had opened the refrigerator door, but stopped before pulling out the pitcher of tea.

"That's right." Abby climbed onto a bar stool, placed one elbow on the tile counter and cupped her chin in her hand.

"But court?" Val knew what the heartache of losing a child could do to a person. As much as she didn't trust Abby, she felt sorry for her right now. Whether Val wanted to admit it or not, in her own way, Abby was a good mother. And there wasn't any question about her loving her kids.

"We're trying to avoid that," Abby said, eyeing a large chocolate layer cake on the counter. The mixing bowls, beaters and spatulas were still soaking in the sink. "I'm having Jeff over tonight to try and patch things up—you know, avoid going to court so that we don't have to put the kids through all that."

"You think it'll work?" She dropped ice into the glasses, poured the tea and then added a wedge of lemon before handing the drink to Abby.

Abby took a long swallow and then twirled the glass, watching the lemon dance in the dark liquid. "Oh, Val, I hope so," she whispered, suddenly pale. "The kids, well, they're everything I have."

"I know."

Taking a sip, Abby sniffed and stood. "Look, I've really got to run. I've got a million things to do. I'm making Jeff dinner and I want it to be perfect. Oh, God, I forgot all about dessert!''

Feeling closer to Abby than she had in a long time, Val smiled. ''Don't worry about it. I baked this cake this afternoon. It's yours if you want it.''

''Are you kidding? Chocolate is Jeff's favorite!'' Abby said.

''Then, it's yours.''

''Oh, Val, thanks. Thanks—for everything!'' She gave her a quick squeeze and accepted the layer cake as she headed for the door.

''I just hope everything works out!''

''So do I,'' Abby said, hurrying outside and smiling to herself as she held on to her treasure. Making peace with Val was already paying off!

Feeling guilty about leaving Richard home to take care of Jason, Laura drove into town toward Trader Vic's restaurant and her meeting with David. Her palms began to sweat, and she was developing a bad case of jitters.

''You're being asinine,'' she told herself. ''It's just a business meeting. And Scooter will be there.'' But she couldn't get rid of the butterflies in her stomach. She rolled down the window and tried to enjoy the evening breeze that caught in her hair as she maneuvered the car through the uneven flow of traffic and stopped at a street light.

The hours at the office had flown by. Now, here she was, keeping an appointment with David Souther. Just the thought of the quiet-spoken, handsome man made her smile and sigh. He was kind, intelligent, successful . . .

But what about Richard? her conscience jeered. Richard. His behavior was driving them farther and farther apart. He'd lost all of his self-confidence and dignity, and was sinking into a hole that was drowning them both. Life with him was no longer fun, and she doubted if they could ever recapture the love they'd once shared.

A horn blasted behind her. "Hey, lady, what're ya waiting for—an invitation?" a gruff voice yelled.

Blushing as she noticed the light was green, Laura stepped on the accelerator and the car sped forward.

She was so nervous that she drove two blocks past the restaurant before realizing her mistake. Managing a quick U-turn, she pulled into the parking lot, got out of the car and handed the young attendant her keys.

"Get your act together," she whispered to herself as she walked through the glass doors and into the dark interior of the restaurant. David and Scooter hadn't arrived yet, so she ducked into the powder room to comb her hair and tamp down her case of nerves. Looking into the mirror, she laughed to herself when she realized that she felt a little like a schoolgirl on a first date. Her cheeks were flushed and her eyes gleamed. "Oh, Laura, don't be a fool," she said before she tossed back her head and lifted her chin. "Well, you're here. You may as well have a good time. This is as good as it gets!" She stuffed her brush back into her purse, shouldered her way out the powder room door and headed for whatever the evening had to offer.

Scooter and David had just walked into the restaurant. David's eyes warmed as she approached, and a lopsided smile tugged at the corners of his mouth.

"Good evening," he said, holding her gaze.

"Glad you made it," Scooter cut in, nervously stuffing his hands into his pockets.

"Glad I came," she replied, glancing from David to Scooter and back again. The maître d' led them to a private table; they ordered champagne and lobster. The dinner was exquisite, and Laura, caught in the celebration, found herself smiling and laughing throughout the meal. She hadn't been so relaxed in months, and her family problems seemed to disappear under the dim lights.

After dinner, as the waiter came around to pour them more coffee, Scooter placed his hand over his cup. "Pass. It's past my bedtime."

"It's only nine-thirty, Scooter," David said, cocking his wrist and checking the time. "The night is young."

"I know, but I'll be a grandfather in less than a month. I've got to start acting my age."

Laura laughed. The trim, happy-go-lucky man sitting across from her looked anything but grandfatherly. "Stick around," she invited.

"Sorry." He put his napkin on the table and stood. He shook David's hand before bending over and kissing Laura on the cheek. "Enjoy yourselves."

Laura watched Scooter leave and felt suddenly awkward and tongue-tied. Being alone with David made her incredibly self-conscious.

"He's a terrific guy," David said, picking up

his water glass and taking a long drink.

"The best."

The silence stretched between them and Laura had trouble meeting David's eyes. David picked up the champagne bottle and poured the last few drops into Laura's glass. "So . . . I've bought a house and lost someone to spend Sundays with. I'm not so sure I like the trade-off," he said.

"You could always start looking for another house," she teased, her eyes dancing.

"No. I like this one."

"It is beautiful."

"The view at night must be spectacular," David murmured, searching her face.

"I thought that's part of what sold you."

David shook his head and grinned. "*You* sold me. You *told* me about the view, remember?"

"That's right. We've never been up there at night, have we?"

"No."

Laura looked into his eyes and pursed her lips. Impulsively, she finished her champagne, all the while ignoring the warnings in the back of her mind. With a flourish she set her empty glass back on the table. "Why don't we have a look?" she suggested.

Sighing, Jeff leaned back on the thick cushions of the L-shaped sofa in Abby's living room. Feeling pleasantly full from a delicious meal, he looked around the room. It was decorated in soft hues of blue and cream—very feminine, very Abby. Here and there she'd added splashes of color: bright pink silk flowers on a corner table, mauve throw pillows on the couch and on the far wall, and her one concession to home and hearth—an old family portrait.

The picture had been taken before the divorce. He had a similar one on his desk in his apartment. Abby had given him the portrait one Christmas— or had it been on Father's Day? He couldn't remember, but then it didn't really matter. He finished off his glass of scotch and heard her talking to herself in the kitchen. Just like old times.

Abby entered the room carrying a pot of coffee and a plate with a thick piece of chocolate cake.

"You remembered," Jeff said, surprised.

"Your favorite. Right?" she said with a grin. Her sparkling blue eyes touched his.

"Right." He felt good all over, warm from the food and the scotch.

She placed the cake on the table and smiled to herself as she poured them each a cup of coffee. So far, so good. Some of the old tricks she'd used to put Jeff in a good mood while they were married still worked. Chocolate cake was one thing he couldn't resist.

Jeff took a bite of the cake. "This is terrific. When did you become such a great baker?"

"The moment I conned Val into baking it for me," she admitted with a shrug. "You know me in the kitchen." She drank some of her coffee and then put her cup back on the table. "Jeff, we're supposed to talk. Iron out our differences."

"I don't know if we can."

"Didn't we decide the kids would be better off with me?"

Jeff stabbed his fork into the remaining cake on his plate and tried to organize his thoughts. He wanted this to come out right for a change. "A year ago, yes."

"So what's changed? I'm saner now than I was then. This is a nice house in a nice neighborhood, with good schools. The kids are happy. What's the problem?"

Jeff's plate clattered to the table and he stood. He felt angry again—cornered. Running his hands through his hair, he walked over to the portrait, fingered the metal frame and leaned against the wall. "This was a lovely evening, Abby. I don't want to ruin it."

"Talk to me calmly, and it won't be ruined. Why do you think the kids would be better off with you?"

He rolled his eyes to the ceiling. "A difference in philosophy. I think parents should be models to their kids."

Nodding her head in agreement, Abby crossed her legs and let her dress hike up, letting her lacy slip peek from under the brilliant red hem. "So do I," she agreed.

Jeff's eyes narrowed. She was so damned beautiful, sitting there pouting. He tried to keep his mind on the conversation, but it was tough. "Then you must think it's setting a good example to have an affair with the married man next door."

"Oh, God, Jeff—"

"You asked me to tell you."

"Do you really think that my private life is something the children are even dimly aware of?" she asked, shocked.

"You'd be surprised how perceptive children are, Abby."

"They can't perceive what's not there for them to see!"

"You're *not* having an affair with him?" Jeff said, cynicism tainting his words.

"It's none of your business whether I am or not."

"I think it is," he threw back at her, pacing to the far side of the room. He coiled and uncoiled a fist, trying to control his rage and the start of a headache at his temples.

Holding up a hand to calm him down, Abby was alarmed to see that she was trembling. Things weren't going as planned, not at all. "Look, Jeff, we were going to discuss the kids."

"We *are* discussing the kids. This is about the kids," he said, his anger rising.

"No, it isn't!"

"Let me ask you something, Abby. When we were married—"

"Oh, Jeff, please."

He glared at her from across the room, took in the provocative glint in her eyes, her unruly blond hair, the deep V of her neckline and the inviting hollow between her breasts. The headache behind his eyes began to pound. "Just how easy were you then? How many neighbors were there?"

"Why are you doing this?"

"Did I know them? Was I a big joke in our circle of friends?" he demanded, his fist crashing against the wall. The portrait slipped and the glass covering the picture cracked.

"That's enough!" Abby slammed her cup onto the coffee table and stood, but Jeff was across the room in an instant. He grabbed her by the arm and yanked her down on the sofa. Then he pinned her shoulders to the cushions and leaned over her.

"How many, Abby?" God, she was making him crazy, Jeff thought, losing all control.

Pushing his face close to hers—so close that she could smell the coffee on his breath, see his pupils dilate, watch a vein pulsing in his forehead—he held her down. His breathing was rapid and shallow, his fingers were digging into her arms, and for the first time, Abby was scared of him.

"Are you still that easy, Abby? Are you still as much fun? Come on Abby, how about a little reunion for old times' sake."

He lowered himself farther, so that his weight rested on her, and his lips fell sloppily against her cheek. Abby twisted and hit him with her fists, but he didn't seem to notice. "Jeff, please, no . . ."

Grabbing her firmly and wrenching her upward, Jeff kissed her—with no love, just cold, calculated, mind-stopping lust. He couldn't think straight, and yet he didn't care. His rage and passion mingled, and all of his thoughts centered on claiming his ex-wife once again.

Abby squirmed beneath him, struggling to get away, making gasping, terrified noises, and Jeff felt a sensation of power he'd never experienced with her. Pushing her farther down on the couch, he held her prisoner. "What differ-

ence could it possibly make to you—one man,
one night, more or less?''

''Jeff, stop it! No!'' she hissed, scratching and
clawing as he settled against her, pinning her
with his weight. ''Don't . . .''

Laura stood in the middle of David's spacious
living room. The huge hillside Tudor house was
empty except for a large drop cloth covering a
workman's ladder and a few cans of paint
stacked in the corners of the room. David tried
the lights, but nothing happened. He lit the single candle on the mantle of the fireplace and
watched Laura as she stared out the window
across the black hills. In the flickering candle-
light her hair glinted with gold highlights, and
her soft peach-colored dress shimmered when
she moved. She was the most beautiful and fas-
cinating woman he'd met in a long, long time.

Laura heard him approach. Staring out at the
impressive view of the city, she wrapped her
arms around herself to fight off the evening
chill.

''You were right. The view is spectacular,''
he said as he placed one arm around her shoulders.

Laura's devil-may-care-attitude at the restaurant
had faded as the champagne wore off. Yet even as
she knew she should pull away from him, she
couldn't. It felt too good to have his arm around
her. Nodding, she turned and surveyed the rest of
the room. ''So,'' she said, trying to break the
thickening silence, ''what are you going to do in
here?'' She shrugged off David's arm and walked
to the center of the room.

"I'm not sure. It's my first house, you know."

"Then everything will be new."

He plunged his hands deep into his pockets. "Yes. I really don't know where to start." David watched Laura move nervously around the room, noted the way she ran her fingers over the gleaming wood of the mantle, saw the worry in her night-darkened eyes.

"I'd start with something special. Something that feels just right to you. Then I'd build on that," she suggested, wishing her voice sounded more normal, less breathless.

"I know what I'd *like* to start with," he said.

Trembling slightly, Laura met his serious gaze. "What?"

He walked toward her, his steps echoing against the hardwood floor. When he reached her, he drew her into the circle of his arms, lowered his head and slowly brushed his lips across hers.

The feel of his mouth against hers was warm and inviting, gentle enough to bring tears to her eyes. When he lifted his head, she could hear her heart thudding wildly in her chest.

"I've waited three months to do that," David said, his voice husky.

"I'm . . . I'm glad."

"That I kissed you?"

"That you waited," she said, her throat dry as she twisted the gold band on her finger—the ring that Richard had given her on their wedding day so many years before.

"Oh." He didn't bother to hide his disappointment.

Laura bit her lip and walked back to the window. What was she doing here alone with David when her home was with Richard and Jason?

David followed after her, then stopped and leaned against the mantle. Feeling like an idiot, he tried to apologize. "Look, I'm sorry. I shouldn't have—"

"No, I . . . I'm glad you did. I wanted to see how it felt."

"And?"

"It felt nice," she admitted. Smiling through the tears gathering in her eyes, she reached for her purse.

"We could build on that."

She shook her head and wiped away her tears. "I can't."

"Why?"

"Because it would be too much for me . . . a relationship that I can't really start. Not now." Laura looked around the empty room again. "The last six months have been . . . chaotic. A lot of changes, good ones. Right now, I feel about my life the way you do about your house: anxious to move in, but not really sure where to start."

"You could start here. Now. With me." He walked over to her and tilted her chin upward with one finger, forcing her to meet the honesty in his clear eyes.

"I've already got something to work with, David. Something to build on—a marriage."

"But what you've said about that—"

"I know. But for the first time, I've realized that Richard needs me. He'd never admit it, but it's true. And, I like being needed. Sure, he's had a hard time dealing with my success, but I know we can work it out. And I want to try.'' Taking a deep breath, Laura realized that she'd finally come to terms with her marriage. ''If I got involved with you, David, I'm afraid I wouldn't have enough left over for Richard.''

''What if nothing's enough?''

''Then it's not enough, but I'll know I tried to do the right thing.'' Laura walked to the front door and opened it.

''You think I could get my deposit back?'' David said, trying to hide his disappointment.

''I doubt it.'' Despite her tears, Laura managed to laugh as she made her way down the brick path leading to the drive.

She was going home. To Richard.

Abby's mind raced as Jeff's weight crushed her to the sofa. She grabbed his hair and yanked with all her might. The searing pain rendered him useless for the split second she needed to escape. Rolling out from under him, Abby clawed the side of his face and then slapped him. ''You bastard,'' she hissed.

Rising to her feet, she towered over him as he lay gasping on the couch, beaten and humiliated.

''Oh, God, Abby.''

''What is the matter with you?'' she choked out, raking her fingers through her hair and trying not to break down completely.

Jeff didn't move.

Winded, Abby stared at him as if he were a stranger. What had gotten into him? He'd been brutal, vicious, horrible! Trying to calm down, she took in several deep breaths and then threw his jacket onto the sofa. "Get out of here, please, Jeff."

He moaned, but didn't try to get up.

"Look, I'm serious, Jeff. I'm going to call Sid if you don't get up and get out of here." When Jeff finally lifted his head, Abby's heart turned over. There was a long scratch on his left cheek, his eyes were red with tears, and though his jaw was clenched, his throat trembled convulsively. He looked absolutely pathetic.

Most of her anger gave way to compassion. Tears blurred her vision. "Why, Jeff? What do you want? What do you really want?"

He tried to speak but couldn't. Ashamed, he looked away from her.

Abby stumbled over some cushions that had fallen to the floor and then sat next to him on the couch. Tenderly touching the scratch beneath his eye, she kissed his cheek. "Tell me, Jeff. What do you really want?"

"It's simple, really . . . I want you back," he whispered hoarsely.

"Oh, Jeff. Poor Jeff." She felt tears slide down her cheeks. Placing her hands on his face, she pulled him forward and cradled his head to her breast. Gently rocking, she held him close.

"Abby?"

"Shhh. Why didn't you say so?"

Jeff looked up into her eyes and saw her smile. Then, she reached behind her head and started lowering the zipper of her dress down her back.

* * *

Awakened by the sound of her own scream, Olivia Cunningham lay frozen in her bed. Her heart was pounding and her breath came in short gasps as she remembered the vivid nightmare.

Throwing off the covers she scrambled out of bed, ran out of her room and down the hallway to Abby's bedroom. Maybe it wasn't a dream after all. Maybe her mother really had left her! Maybe she'd taken Brian with her!

Heart thudding, tears streaming down her face, she didn't bother with the lights but ran into the room and flung herself on the bed. "Mommy—"

Jeff sat up with a start. "Olivia, what's wrong?"

Olivia jumped off the bed and backed up against the wall. She hadn't expected to hear a man's voice, see a male shape in the bed. In the dark room, she didn't recognize Jeff, couldn't see Abby. Panicking, she began to cry. "Where's my mom?"

"She's asleep, honey. Come here. I'll hold you. It's Daddy." He fumbled for the light, couldn't find it, and then reached for his daughter.

"No! I want her. Mommy!" Bewildered and scared, Olivia ran around to the other side of the bed. Desperate to find Abby, she started yanking off the covers. "Mommy!"

Abby groaned. Rubbing her eyes, she felt Olivia cuddle up beside her. "Olivia?" she said groggily. "What's wrong?"

"I'll take care of it," Jeff said. Disturbed by

Olivia's reaction to him, he wanted to make things right again.

"No! I want my mommy . . ." Olivia cried, holding tightly to Abby.

"It's okay, baby. Mommy's here. Everything's all right," Abby whispered, softly stroking Olivia's hair.

Gradually Olivia calmed down and started to breathe normally again. She held on to her mother possessively but peeked over Abby's shoulder to Jeff. What was he doing here—in her mommy's bed?

Abby finally got out of bed, picked up her daughter and headed out of the room.

"Want a hand?" Jeff asked.

She shook her head. Olivia was nearly asleep again. She probably wouldn't remember much about the nightmare in the morning, and Abby didn't want to risk any complicated questions about Jeff.

Placing Olivia back in her bed, Abby smiled down at her. In the dim illumination from the night light, Olivia looked a lot like Jeff. Tonight, Abby was feeling good about him. After the brutal scene on the couch, he'd been a tender and gentle lover.

Sitting on the edge of Olivia's bed, she stroked her daughter's long hair.

Olivia stirred but didn't open her eyes. "Did you and Daddy make up, Mommy?" she mumbled.

Abby shook her head and looked out the window. A silver crescent moon hung low in the sky. "We're not arguing, honey. We just decided not to be married, remember? I explained that to you and Brian.''

''So why's he staying overnight?''

Abby sighed and leaned back against Olivia's headboard. ''We're still friends. And sometimes we still need each other,'' she said.

Olivia snuggled against the pillows. ''I think he's unhappy when he's alone.''

''Probably,'' Abby agreed, feeling a little contrite. ''He doesn't have you guys to keep him from being lonely.''

''I think he should remarry.''

Abby stared down at her daughter in amazement and watched as Olivia wriggled down into the covers and tucked the pillow under her chin.

''Would you stay in here with me for a while, Mom? In case I have bad dreams again?''

''Of course, honey.''

''You can't snore, though,'' Olivia murmured jokingly before drifting off to sleep.

Abby slid lower on the bed and placed her arm around Olivia until the child was breathing regularly. Somewhere in the darkness, Olivia's rabbit stirred in its cage, and then the house was quiet again.

As she stared up at the ceiling, thinking about Jeff and the fact that he was only a few feet down the hall, Abby couldn't help but wonder what would happen in the morning.

Laura opened the front door and heard the television blaring from the family room. The noise was loud enough to wake the dead, let alone the neighbors. How in the world could Jason sleep through it?

Racing down the hall, she found Richard sprawled across the sofa. Despite the din, he was sound asleep. She dropped her purse on the table, shut off the television and stared at her husband. He was dressed in torn jeans and no shirt. One arm was flung over the couch, the other across his eyes. He hadn't shaved since morning, and stubble darkened the lower half of his face. His mouth was open and slack, and he was snoring in drunken oblivion.

On the floor next to him were two empty liquor bottles.

Laura felt like crying. This broken man had once been her proud, self-assured husband.

Fighting a losing battle with tears, she sat down and gently shook him. He snored more loudly and attempted to roll over. She tried again, this time shaking him harder.

"Richard . . . Richard, wake up."

He snorted and closed his mouth.

"Wake up!" Gently, she slapped the side of his face.

Richard stirred, carefully lifting one eyelid to discover the source of the annoyance. Seeing Laura, he was confused. He bolted upright. "What? God, is something wrong?" He pushed his hair out of his eyes and tried to focus.

"Honey, wake up. Let's go to bed."

Richard rubbed his eyes. Every muscle in his body ached and his head throbbed. What the hell had happened? When had Laura gotten home? Where was Johnny Carson?

He opened and closed his eyes before finally waking up enough to take in the whole situation. Grimacing at the foul taste in his mouth and the mess on the floor, he tried to get up, failed miserably, and finally grabbed Laura's arm for support.

"Maybe I'll just stay down here," he said, his voice rough and gritty.

"And wake up feeling even worse in the morning? Come on, I'll give you a hand."

He stared at her for a long moment and then tried to smile. It didn't quite come off right, but Laura didn't care. With her arm around his waist, they struggled up the stairs. Together.

Chapter Nine
The Morning After

The sky was an unusually hazy, leaden shade of gray as Val cut the single white rose from her garden. She paused to smell the fragrant bud and then hurried through the back door and into the kitchen. Slipping the flower into a crystal bud vase, she set the solitary rose on the table next to a large platter of ham, eggs, and hash browned potatoes.

"What's this?" Gary asked as he came into the room. His hair was still wet from the shower and his brows were pulled together in fierce concentration. His cheeks were hollow and the corners around his mouth were pinched; whatever was eating at him had given him a tense, almost haggard appearance, Val thought. "Don't tell me it's a special occasion that I forgot?"

"Nope. Just a peace offering," Val said with a smile. "Come on, eat before it gets cold."

"Wait a minute." He rubbed his chin and

stared thoughtfully at his wife. "I didn't know we were at war."

"We aren't . . . not really," she said, pouring coffee. "I just wanted to make up for the other night. You know, because of what happened at Abby's party. Remember?"

"How could I forget?"

"Abby and I called a truce yesterday; I thought I'd better do the same here."

Gary placed his elbows on the table and studied his wife. "Hold on a minute. What did you say? You and Abby—a truce?"

"I guess that's what you'd call it."

"Why?"

Val shrugged and wondered again if she'd been conned by Abby. "I felt sorry for her."

"We *are* talking about Abby Cunningham, right?"

"Of course we are," she snapped. "Abby came over here yesterday to apologize about the way J.R. acted at her house, and then she explained about Jeff and the kids."

"What about them?" He began eating, but didn't take his eyes off her.

"You don't know?"

"Know *what* ?"

"That he's suing her for custody," Val said. "Custody of the children."

Gary's face tensed and his lips formed a tight line as he buttered a slice of toast.

"You really didn't know, did you?"

"Why would I?"

Val sipped her coffee. "I just thought she might have said something to you at work."

"Nope. First I've heard of it," he muttered.

"Do you believe it?"

"I guess so—but Jeff didn't strike me as the type to put his kids through a court battle."

"You liked him?"

Gary shrugged. "Yeah. He was okay. But what does it have to do with us?"

Val smiled. "Nothing, really. I just understood Abby's concern about her children. I know what it's like to lose one."

Gary placed his hand over hers. "That's all behind us now."

"Is it, Gary?" she asked, her blue eyes pleading. "I just can't believe that J.R. is in Knots Landing just for that oil convention. He's got something up his sleeve—I can smell it. It has something to do with Sid's new car, doesn't it? You're into some deal involving Sid's new engine design."

"Of course not! Sid's car has nothing to do with J.R.!"

"Then why is he here? Something's going on!"

"You're imagining things! I told you that I wasn't involved with J.R., and I meant it. As for Sid's car, it's his baby. No one else, including J.R., has anything to do with it!" He set his fork on his plate and didn't bother with the rest of the meal. Scraping his chair back, he got up from the table. "Look, I'm late. I'll see ya later." And then he was off without so much as a good-bye. Val heard the back door slam and the truck roar out of the driveway. Then the oppressive silence of being alone in the house settled upon her.

She tried to shrug off the gloomy feeling, but

couldn't. She couldn't forget that it was J.R. who had ruined her life all those years ago, J.R. who had taken Lucy away, J.R. who was in Knots Landing dragging Lucy's name through the mud and somehow getting involved with Gary.

Well, it wouldn't happen again. Not as long as there was a breath of life in her body. She got up from the table, set the dishes in the sink, and glanced at the single white rose on the table before running upstairs to change.

Abby yawned and stretched in her bed. It felt great to sleep in for a change. She heard the clanging of dishes, pots and pans coming from the kitchen; Jeff was already hard at work. Smiling, she got up, ran her fingers through her hair, and tossed on her robe. Then she went downstairs to the kitchen, where she found Jeff busily cleaning up the breakfast dishes and straightening up the mess the kids had left behind.

Dressed in gray sweat pants and a T-shirt, he was scrubbing the sink and looking as if he actually enjoyed the awful project.

"You had a change of clothes?" she asked.

"Yeah—in the trunk. I thought I'd go to the club this morning and work out."

"Oh." Smiling to herself, Abby poured herself a cup of coffee before she dropped into one of the kitchen chairs and unfolded the morning paper. After skimming the headlines on the front page, she turned to the women's section to check out the latest fashions trends and local gossip.

Jeff began whistling. Shaking her head, Abby took a sip of the piping hot coffee.

"I fed the kids, got them dressed and made their lunches," he said, folding the dishcloth and setting it on the counter.

Abby didn't look up. "Thanks."

Jeff hoisted himself onto the counter, let his legs swing in front of the cupboards, and stared down at her. "What do they normally do? If I hadn't been here—"

"I'd have been up," Abby finished for him. "This morning I knew you'd be down here." Glancing at him, she grinned and winked. "You're predictable."

"Someone has to take care of things," he snapped.

"Like I said . . . predictable," she mumbled to herself and then flipped to the movie section.

Jeff started to defend himself but stopped short. "You know," he said, watching the way she licked her finger before turning the page, "when I started making breakfast, it was just like old times. Olivia wanted pancakes, Brian started yelling for waffles. We finally compromised . . . waffles this time, and pancakes the next."

Abby cocked her head and lifted her brow. "Next time?" she repeated.

"Yeah. The next time we have breakfast together."

Inwardly sighing, she refolded the paper and then went over to the stove to pour herself another cup of coffee. Returning to the table, she braced herself against the edge and met his eyes. "Jeff, I meant what I said last night.

The two of us would never work."

"We did last night." His eyes twinkled and his lips turned up at the corners.

"One night's hardly the basis for a marriage."

"It's a start," he insisted.

"It's not a start . . . or a finish. It's one night."

His smile faded. "Clever, Abby. Invite me over to talk, get me into bed, and everything's suddenly fine, right? Everything's forgotten," he sneered, all his kind feelings for her turning to dust as he realized she'd used him all over again. And he'd stupidly, blindly, even eagerly let her!

"Stop it, Jeff. I didn't make you do anything. And you got exactly what you wanted all along . . . *me!*"

"That's not enough!"

"You were the one who dozed off," she said, her eyes turning cold.

Jeff blushed, and felt a headache coming on full force. "You're disgusting."

"At least I'm honest. All your hypocritical concern for the kids disappeared like—" she snapped her fingers "—*that* last night when you realized that we might end up in bed."

He jumped off the counter and took one of the kitchen chairs. Swinging it around, he straddled it and faced her. "What happened to you, Abby?" he asked, his eyes piercing hers. "You're not the woman I married ten years ago."

"The perfect Mrs. Cunningham?" she threw back at him. "I never was. The only place she existed was in your head, Jeffrey. And that's exactly what you can't stand. The fact that I'm something other than your fantasy. Take it or leave it, like it or not, I'm *me*!"

"I'll leave it," he said flatly as he pushed the chair back and stood. Glaring down at her, he felt the veins in his neck begin to throb. How one woman could make him so crazy was incomprehensible, but then it had always been that way between him and Abby. Love and hate, hot and cold.

Abby met his gaze and didn't flinch. "I'm going to fight you every inch of the way, Jeff, and you're going to lose. All the way around—in court, with me, and with the kids." She walked over to the sink and poured her coffee down the drain.

"We'll see, Abby. We'll see," he said evenly before walking through the house and out the front door.

Abby felt her stomach knot. It wasn't like Jeff to be so cold and calm. He was planning something; she could feel it.

"Oh, God, what now?" Slumping against the wall she looked around the clean kitchen. In one corner of the counter was the remainder of Val's chocolate cake. Abby's lips twisted into a cynical smile. A lot of good the cake had done her. Without stopping to examine her motives, Abby crossed the room, picked it up, and threw it into the garbage can under the sink.

"Take that, you bastard!" Then she straightened and wiped her hands on her robe. "Okay, Jeff," she said out loud, "whatever you're planning, I'm ready!"

* * *

Michael Fairgate finished his breakfast early and left the table mumbling a quiet "'scuse me."

Karen looked at his plate, realized he hadn't eaten anything, and began to worry all over again. She looked at Diana, who just shrugged indifferently.

While Karen cleared the dishes, Michael wandered into the living room. Once there, he felt the same old tension begin to build. He sat down and his leg bounced up and down. To relieve the energy bursting inside him, he stood and began tossing a ball into the air with one hand, attempting to catch it with the other and having very little success at either.

Maybe I am a freak, he thought. *I can't even catch the stupid ball.*

Discouraged, he looked into the mirror, made a face at himself, and flopped onto his mother's favorite antique chair.

Karen stood in the doorway and watched Michael as he continued to toss the ball from one hand to the other.

"Michael?"

He nearly jumped out of his skin. "What?"

"Need some company?"

"Naw." He looked up at her, scrambled out of her good chair and shrugged. "Well, maybe."

"I thought so." Smiling, Karen walked into the room and placed one arm around his shoulders. "Come on, sit down, it's okay." Seeing his worried look, she grinned. "Really. I won't bite—even if you were on Grandma's chair."

"Sorry."

"It's okay. Now, why aren't you ready? I thought you and I were going running this morning."

He looked away from her and bit his lip. "I don't feel like it."

"What do you mean you don't feel like it? I've got you down for eight laps," she teased. What was wrong with Michael? For the past couple of days he'd been depressed. At first she'd passed it off as the aftereffects of his fight with Diana, but there was more to it; she could see the sadness in his eyes. Any attempt she'd made to reach him the past few days had been an exercise in futility.

This morning, however, she was determined to get to the root of the problem.

"I don't like to run," he said.

"Oh, sure."

"Really, Mom."

"What are you talking about? You love to run."

"But . . . but you shouldn't have to go running with me. It isn't fair to you."

"Don't be silly, Michael. I love it," she said, giving him a heart-felt squeeze. "Come on, sport, give. What's all this talk about not wanting to run? And I want straight answers, okay?"

Michael slid out of her arms and fought the urge to cry. "I heard you and Daddy talking the other night," he whispered, his lower lip trembling. "I . . . I don't want to be a freak!"

Karen was stunned. "You're not! That's not what we said—"

"It is!" he shouted. "I heard you!"

"Oh, Michael," she said with a sigh. It was too late to call back the horrid word. Unfortunately, the damage had been done. She looked down at her hands before meeting her son's anxious eyes. "We shouldn't have used the word. It was wrong and stupid. Michael, we love you."

"I know, but you're always fighting about me these days," he retorted, tears beginning to drizzle down his cheeks.

Karen was dying inside. The last thing she'd ever meant to do was hurt Michael; he'd been through so much already. "Honey, don't talk like that."

"But it's true. Diana's always mad at me, and you and Daddy and Eric have to keep me busy all the time."

"Hey! You've got an illness. We're all pitching in because we want to. What's wrong with that?"

"Plenty," he retorted, sniffing and trying to swallow back his tears. "All I am is trouble."

"No way! Listen, Michael, you're a terrific kid—with your own personal energy crisis. In reverse. You've got too much of it. So big deal. So we play ball with you, run you around the track a few times, swim, do what we can to help you work it off. That doesn't make you a freak."

"It still makes me more trouble than I'm worth."

"Worth? Are you kidding? You're mine, aren't you? That makes you one of the most valuable people around. I don't give birth to second-rate people," she said, smiling through her own blur of tears.

Michael swiped at his face and forced a self-conscious grin. His mother's reassurances were starting to work their magic on him. He felt better than he had in a long time.

"Okay?" Karen put her hands on her knees and stood. "End of lecture. Your father and I may disagree about a lot of things, but not about this. We're your parents. A team. You can count on us. There's no such thing as your being too much trouble for us. And I don't want to hear any arguments about it. Got it?"

Michael nodded and got to his feet. "Got it!"

Tousling his hair, Karen walked to the front door. "So, are you up for your eight laps today?"

"How about ten?"

Karen rolled her eyes to the ceiling. "I had to go and open my big mouth!"

Laughing together, they headed out the door into the bright morning sunshine.

Jeff tried to control the quiet rage that burned deep in his gut.

He'd been used by Abby and all he could think about was getting even with her. Though he'd been calm when he'd walked out of her house, he now felt as though he couldn't drive away without first plotting his revenge. He had spent the last five minutes pacing up and down her driveway, letting off steam and wanting to strangle her.

He was still furious when he saw Karen and Michael, their arms linked together, hurry out of the Fairgate house. Their happiness only served to drive home how rotten his own life was. Wanting to make tracks before he was spotted, he unlocked the car door and started to get in. Just then he heard Karen yell his name.

"Damn!" he muttered, crashing his fist against the roof of the car.

"Hey, Jeff!" Karen called from across the street.

Just what he needed, his goody-two-shoes of a sister-in-law—his *ex*-sister-in-law—butting in.

Karen started to run across the street, but stopped. Seeing the set of Jeff's jaw, she turned to Michael and tried to come up with an excuse to talk to Jeff alone. There wasn't one. "Wait here for just a second, honey. I want to talk to Jeff for a minute. Okay?"

"Sure." Michael jogged back to their house, went into the garage, grabbed his basketball and began shooting baskets.

Dashing across the street, Karen decided to meet Jeff straight on. "Hi."

His stare was cold and distant. "Hello, Karen," he said with a smirk. "And, yes, I spent the night."

"Oh." Feeling awkward, she glanced at Abby's house.

"Is that all you wanted to know?" he asked. "I'm in kind of a hurry."

In for a penny, in for a pound, Karen decided. She directed her gaze back at Jeff. His expression hadn't changed, but a muscle was twitching in the corner of his jaw. "Well, Abby told us about the custody suit, and, frankly, we were shocked that it had gone that far."

"I'm late for work, Karen," he lied.

"Look, what I'm trying to say is that I hope that I didn't encourage you to do anything—"

"Foolish? Like fight for my own kids?" he mocked.

Karen looked up at the gray sky and sighed. If only she could reach him. "No one wins in a custody battle, Jeff. Not really."

"And blood's thicker than water, isn't it? She is Sid's little sister, after all."

"Oh, Jeff, I'm talking for myself right now, but I know that Sid wants what's best for both of you."

"Sure." he crossed his arms over his chest and cocked his head in the direction of the Fairgate house. "You, Sid, Abby—you're all part of the same conspiracy. You invite me to dinner, whisper one thing in my ear. She takes me to bed and whispers something else. And then I end up getting ripped off by both of you."

By the time he'd finished, Karen's eyes were blazing. She was furious—but not at the confused man in front of her. It was all too obvious that Abby had manipulated him again, and now they were all paying the price; especially Olivia and Brian. "Jeff, that's not true."

"No?"

"No, of course not! Jeff, please, just listen a minute, okay? You know that a custody battle would be terrible for the children, don't you?"

Jeff didn't move.

"Don't you?"

Rubbing the tension from his shoulders, he avoided her gaze. "Yes."

"But you're still going through with it?" she asked in disbelief.

His chin thrust out, Jeff refused to answer.

"Jeff?"

Letting out a deep breath, he shook his head. "No, I'm not going through with it," he admitted. Slowly his plan was forming, a plan that would set things straight once and for all.

Elated, Karen threw her arms around him. "Oh, Jeff, I knew it." Kissing him, she let out a long sigh of relief. "I told Sid that when the chips were down you wouldn't sacrifice the kids. It wouldn't be fair."

"*This* isn't fair," he said quietly.

"What?"

"My going home now . . . alone . . . away from my kids."

"But you just said—"

"I know. No court fight. That's what I said. I didn't say anything about fair play," he reminded her.

"I don't understand." Karen took a step backward and noticed the gleam of determination in his eyes, the hardening of his expression.

Then his countenance changed suddenly, and his eyes glinted as if he'd just realized he'd given too much away. "There's nothing to understand, I'm just letting off steam. Bye, Karen." He opened the car door and slid inside. Within seconds the engine roared to life and he backed out of Abby's driveway.

Feeling helpless, she stood in the street while his car roared away from the cul-de-sac. She felt uneasy about his parting remarks, and couldn't shake the sense that something horrible was about to happen.

"You're imagining things," she told herself as she waved to Michael and started to jog down the street. But Jeff's warning echoed in her heart: *I didn't say anything about fair play.*

What the devil did he mean?

Ginger puttered around her empty house and tried to brighten her outlook on life.

So she was pregnant. So she was divorcing her husband. So what?

Frowning, she looked around the house. Since Kenny had moved out, there was more room than she needed or wanted. Nothing drove this point home like cleaning day.

Pushing the heavy vacuum cleaner around from room to room, she was oblivious to anything but the steady droning of the motor and the feel of new life inside her. Lost in thought, she didn't hear the front door bell chime.

As she maneuvered around the bedroom doorway, she stretched the limits of the electrical cord, and suddenly the machine went dead. The ringing door bell pealed through the house.

She glanced at the clock. Nine-thirty. Who'd be coming over so early? Rubbing her aching back, she made her way to the front door and opened it. On the porch—wearing his outlandish leather pants and his shirt opened to his navel—was her husband. He had a cowboy hat tilted back on his head and was carrying a huge stuffed panda with a bright red ribbon tied around its neck.

"Kenny . . ." Taken aback, she just stood in the doorway. "You're the last person I expected—"

"Surprise!" He placed the stuffed animal in her arms and slid past her into the house.

"Not again . . ."

When she shut the door, he turned and faced her. A huge smile swept across his face and he pushed the brim of his Stetson even further back. "I did it, babe. I broke up with Sylvie."

Ginger was too flabbergasted to respond.

Kenny beamed proudly and sauntered into the living room. He sat in his favorite chair and propped his boots up on the coffee table as he stared up at his wife. "I moved out of her house, just like you wanted me to."

Ginger couldn't find her voice. Staring at him from the entry hall, she leaned against the banister leading upstairs and put the stuffed animal on the floor.

Kenny lifted his palms skyward. "What's the matter? I thought you'd be happy. It's just you and me, babe—like we both want it to be."

"Wait a minute," she said, finally understanding the meaning behind his grandiose theatrics. "Are you thinking that you're going to move back in here?"

"Well, you always said that when I left Sylvie . . ."

". . . we'd talk. *Talk.* I didn't say you could move from her house back into mine!"

Suddenly, Ginger felt an unwelcome attack of nausea. She paled and grabbed onto the banister for support.

Kenny was beside her in an instant, but he

didn't notice her ashen complexion or the slight rounding of her abdomen under her jeans. He was too intent on wrapping his arms around her and staring into her eyes.

Ginger tried to squirm away, but his arms tightened.

Though slight, he was strong and determined. "Come on, babe, you don't belong with anybody else but me."

"Oh, is that what this is about?" she said, finally slipping out of his grasp and walking into the living room.

"What?"

Shaking her head, Ginger told herself she'd always been a fool for him. Maybe she still was. "For months I've been asking you to move out of Sylvie's, and all you could talk about was your big career with her. Now that I've started seeing somebody else, suddenly you're ready to move back in. What about your career now?"

Kenny walked up behind her and put his arms over her shoulders. His breath fanned her hair, and Ginger shifted away from him. "Okay, I admit it. I can't stand seeing you with another guy. What's wrong with that?"

She wheeled to face him. "What's wrong is that there's more to it. You're always showing up with presents and pizzas—kid's stuff—expecting that toys and munchies will make everything all right. I'm not a child, Kenny. You've got to grow up." Without realizing it, she rubbed her slightly swollen abdomen. They would both have to grow up, and soon.

"I don't want to grow up. I just want you

back." He reached forward, touched a lock of her fiery red hair and let it fall back into place.

Closing her eyes, Ginger tried to forestall the headache beginning to pound at the base of her skull. "Kenny, it's more complicated than that."

"Why does it have to be complicated? I love you. You love me—you know you do. All I want is for you and me to be together. Alone. Just the two of us."

God, he was so simple. "It can't *be* like that anymore," she nearly shouted.

"Why not?"

Hesitating for a second, she searched his eyes and considered telling him about the baby, the fact that he was going to be a father, but she couldn't. Not yet. "It just can't, that's all," she whispered, her throat suddenly tight.

Shattered, Kenny stepped away from her. He squared his hat on his head and hiked up his pants. "You know, I thought you'd be happy. I thought this was what you wanted."

"Oh, Kenny, I wish it were as simple as you want it to be," she said, wrapping her arms around herself.

"It could be," he said, heading toward the door. "But you won't let it."

He swaggered out the front door and let it slam shut behind him. Ginger watched as he jumped into his sports car, threw it into reverse and squealed out of the driveway. Then she looked back to the entry hall and saw the huge panda at the bottom of the stairs.

Tears began to slide down her cheeks.

* * *

Leafing through a thick stack of documents, J.R. leaned back in his chair, crossed his booted feet on the desk and listened to the inane excuses on the other end of the line.

"It's not complicated, Quigley," he cut in, his even Texan drawl uncompromising and sarcastic. "I'm sure even you can comprehend it. We've got the drilling rights, and they want 'em. That puts us on the high ground. So don't do something asinine at the negotiations, like cave-in."

J.R. frowned. He loved the back-dealing and one-upmanship that characterized the oil industry in Dallas; he knew the game well and was a master player. And it bugged the living hell out of him when the pawns weren't doing what they were told to.

There was a loud knock on his hotel room door. The pounding interrupted his train of thought, but he was tired of arguing with the idiot on the other end of the line, anyway. "Quigley, I've got to go. Call me around four and let me know how it went."

Tossing the phone into its cradle, J.R. stood up and walked across the thick carpet. He paused for a minute at the mirror, straightened his tie, smoothed back his hair and then finally swung open the door to face a beautiful but stern-looking woman.

Val.

The morning had just gone from bad to worse.

J.R. recovered in time to bow slightly and grin. "Valene. Well, what do you know? I *am* honored."

Val met the mockery in his blue eyes. "I'd like to talk to you, J.R."

"By all means."

Ushering her into the room and offering her a seat, he attempted to size up the woman's mental state. He could sense her nervousness but couldn't quite put his finger on what it was that had motivated her to a showdown with him this morning. In the past, she'd always run from him like a scared rabbit.

But she was older now and, from the looks of her, stronger.

"Val, may I order you up a drink?" he said, reaching for the phone. "Or maybe some milk?"

Ignoring the insinuation, Val managed to hold on to her composure. She folded her hands in her lap. "I want to talk to you about Gary."

J.R. leered. "Something wrong with Gary?"

"He promised me he wouldn't make any deals with you."

"I see. And you're here to make sure that he keeps his word."

"I want to know, J.R. I want to know what you're getting my husband into," she said.

He had tolerated her intrusion with hopes of some amusement. He'd always loved to bait good old Val. But he was growing weary of the game. "Honey, I'm not getting your husband into anything. The closest I've even gotten to a Ewing since I left Dallas is right here and now."

"I care about my husband. I love him."

"Valene, you're a really pretty woman, but

you give me a pain where I have to sit down."

"Good!" She stood and walked to the window. In the distance she could see the ocean. Instead of being a clear blue, it reflected the gray of the sky.

"Gary's never succeeded too much in life," J.R. said slowly, stretching to his full height before joining her at the window. "You know why? It's 'cause of you."

"What?" She turned all of her attention back to her brother-in-law.

"You think small, Valene. Small. He's got a noose around his neck and you're hanging on the end of it, dragging him down."

She wondered why she'd bothered to come to J.R.'s room. She'd been desperate, panicked—but coming here had been a big mistake. "You're a vile, evil man," she whispered. "I believe you'd do anything to ruin other people's lives."

"And I believe our conversation just ended."

Val saw the anger burning in his eyes and she smiled. "One of these days someone is going to pay you back for all you've done. Don't be surprised if that someone is me." Then she stalked out of the room, leaving the door wide open.

J.R. watched her exit and then closed the door. Valene had certainly developed a backbone. About time. Now, if she could ever find some brains to go with that new spine of hers, she might just be able to hold onto Gary.

Unless, of course, Abby Cunningham made her move first.

Chapter Ten

Parting Shots

A red Porsche sat on a side street near Knots Landing Motors. It was partially hidden by four lanes of traffic and didn't attract too much attention.

The two men seated in the front of the flashy car smoked cigarettes as they listened to a lively country tune on the radio. Without speaking, they watched the employees of Knots Landing Motors slowly leave the building.

Roy Lance rubbed his jaw, but his dark eyes were trained on the front of the building. Smoke curled lazily up from the cigarette dangling from his mouth.

Frank Korshak watched the back door, and his lips twisted into a smile at the sight of Gary Ewing's empty pickup. The snake was still inside.

"Haven't seen anyone for five minutes," Roy said impatiently.

"Just a few more minutes. We want to be

sure," Frank said. He lit another cigarette, squinted his eyes against the smoke and leaned back in his seat. He was enjoying the wait. Nothing gave him more of a high than issuing warnings to deadbeat customers.

When Frank saw Sid leave the building and lock the doors, he felt the adrenaline begin to pump through his veins. "Okay, this is it. Let's go." He threw the butt of his cigarette out the open window, switched off the radio, pocketed the keys and opened the door.

Dashing across the rush-hour traffic, both men approached the building according to plan. They moved quickly to the shop door and nervously surveyed the surrounding area. Finding the door locked, Roy pulled a small tool kit from his coat pocket and picked the lock easily.

Frank grinned. "You go around front. Maybe he's in the showroom."

Roy edged along the wall to the front of the building while Frank slipped inside the unlocked door. Peering into the shop, he noted the smell of grease and oil, and the tools neatly arranged beside the cars that had been left in various stages of repair, but he heard nothing. No one was around. He checked the men's room, a side office, and the parts department, but found no one. Then he turned his attention to the front offices and the showroom.

Gary Ewing was in the building, and Frank couldn't wait to catch up to him. His fingers itched for the feel of his scrawny neck.

Gary rubbed his eyes. It had been a long day. The argument with Val still weighed heavily on his mind, and then there was the matter of the money—the money that Frank and Roy wanted, the money he didn't have, the money amounting to fifty thousand dollars.

He snapped his briefcase shut and walked past Abby's office. She was still inside; he could hear the calculator keys clicking as she worked on the books.

"Working late?" he asked, sticking his head through the doorway before slipping inside.

She looked up and smiled, that brilliant Abby smile that lit up her blue eyes and gave her face a special glow. "Yeah. I got in late this morning."

"Val said you were having a little trouble with Jeff."

"Make that a lot," she said.

"I'm sorry. I know how much the kids mean to you."

"We'll work it out," she said.

"You're sure?"

"No, but I'm still working on it."

"Good." He stepped toward the door, but her sharp whisper stopped him.

"Gary?"

When he turned he saw the panic in her eyes as she motioned to the window. Outside, everything looked normal—and then he saw the red car. Fear slid down his spine and every muscle in his body coiled. "Stay here," he whispered. "I'll take care of this."

"Don't. Gary. Wait—" She reached for his arm, but he shook her off and pushed her up against the wall.

His eyes glinted with blue fire. "Stay here,

Abby," he warned. "This is my problem." He
let go of her, quietly opened the door to the
hall, and then locked it behind him. If anyone
wanted to get to Abby, they'd have to break
down the door.

Frank slunk into the showroom and found it to
be as quiet as the other parts of the building.
He looked around and walked slowly between
the shiny new models. Roy wasn't in sight; neither was Gary Ewing. He did a quick check out
the window. The pickup hadn't moved.

Smiling, he walked over to the door leading
to the offices. As he reached for the knob, the
door burst open and pinned him to the wall.
Gary Ewing was right behind it, pushing hard.

Startled, his breath knocked out of his lungs,
Frank stumbled back from behind the door. "I
thought you'd still be here," he growled, ball-
ing a fist and slamming it into Gary's ribs.

Without a word Gary clenched his fingers
around Frank's neatly pressed lapels and then
shoved him back against the wall. Frank's head
cracked against the concrete.

"Hey, wait a minute," Frank said, his face
red, his fists pounding against Gary's abdomen.

But Gary didn't let up and shoved again, a
sick feeling of power flowing through him
when Frank groaned and stopped battering
him. "*You* wait a minute, *pal*!"

Frank shook his head, lifted his eyes, then
started to smile. Turning, Gary followed the
goon's gaze and saw Roy Lance through the
plate glass. He was trying without a lot of suc-

cess to pick the lock on the front door.

Realizing that Roy would be on him in a minute, Gary clenched his teeth. His eyes darted across the showroom as he tried to figure out how to handle both men at once. Two on one. The odds weren't very good.

"Call him off," he hissed at Frank, shoving the man hard again.

But Frank just smiled, a lop-sided grin that showed off the gold crowns in his mouth. "No way, *pal*. Me and Roy, we've been waitin' for this all week. . . ."

Abby stared at the phone and tried to quiet the panic that was making her heart thud wildly. In a few minutes Sid would be home. Maybe Karen was there—she could give him the message. But then they'd know about the stolen parts scam. And it might be too late, anyway. Gary might already be beaten up, maybe killed!

Pacing between the phone and the window, she felt her insides shred. Then, swallowing her fear and ignoring Gary's warning, she slipped her letter opener and her heaviest paperweight into her purse. Her heart in her throat, she slid quietly through the door of her office and began inching her way along the wall of the hall leading to the showroom. She was scared beyond belief, but she knew that she had to try and help Gary.

She cringed when she heard the front door bang open. Dear God, they were inside! There was a scuffle of feet, and then silence. Shaking, she walked into the showroom.

* * *

Frank burst through the service area doors trying to elude Gary. But the younger man was
right on his heels. Looking around for a place
to hide, Frank jumped over some tires; he also
rolled over a battery charger and tried to push
any spare parts he could find behind him in
order to trip Gary.

But Gary was acting on an instinct that told
him that the best defense was a good offense.
He dodged the wrench that Frank threw at him
and then leapt over a stack of tires as he lunged
for the burly henchman. His arms circled
Frank's thick waist as he tackled him. They
both went sprawling down in a heap of black
rubber and crashed into a car jack. Gary felt a
fist smash against his jaw, but he managed to
roll on top of Frank, press the hood's face into
the concrete floor and wrench his left arm
behind his back.

The bigger man screamed in pain; Gary
twisted his arm upward and felt the sickening
yank of tendons ripping. Frank swore and
writhed in agony, but Gary wouldn't let up.

"Whoa! Wait a minute," Frank pleaded.

Hearing the noise, Abby ran down the corri-
dor not knowing what she would find. Her
heart raced as she pictured Gary, broken and
bleeding, lying on the cold concrete.

Frank attempted to stop Gary again. "Cut it
out, kid. I wasn't going to hurt you."

"Yeah, sure you weren't. You're my best
buddy. Ain't that right, pal?"

Roy broke through the back door and saw
that Gary had somehow gotten Frank down.
Jesus, nothing was going right, he thought. He

slunk behind a workbench, close enough to see Frank's face. "Frank!"

Gary's head snapped up and Frank tried to get away. Together they rolled around on the ground and crashed into a pile of tires, which then came tumbling down on them. Gary slipped his arm around the big man's neck and had him in a choke hold when Abby, looking scared out of her wits, stumbled into the service area.

"Gary! Oh, God . . ."

Roy heard her scream and quickly changed direction.

Stumbling backward, Abby tripped and couldn't get away.

Roy was on her in a flash. Grabbing her and wrapping an arm around her neck, Roy half carried her, half dragged her toward the battle.

Abby screamed and tried to bite the big man's arm. "Gary!" she choked out. She kicked at Roy's shins but he tightened his grip around Abby's neck and his small eyes gleamed in pleasure when she moaned.

"Let him go, Ewing," he said.

Gary looked up to see Abby's dress torn and hiked up, her face drained of all color. Roy squeezed just a little tighter and Abby winced in pain.

Knowing he had just run out of options, Gary released Frank, who slid to the floor.

Roy didn't move.

"Smart boy," Frank said, rubbing his jaw and getting to his feet.

"Not smart enough, though," Roy taunted.

Feeling helpless, Gary stood, shoulders tense,

ready to lunge at both men if they didn't let
Abby go.

Frank brushed himself off and offered a
bruised grin to his tormentor. His hard eyes
narrowed with new respect. "Not bad. You
caught me off guard. But you got it all wrong,
Gary. We just came by to talk to you. To
remind you about tomorrow. Payday. Talk.
That's all." Glancing at Roy, he motioned with
his hands and frowned. "Let her go."

Roy released Abby.

"We'll be back. Tomorrow."

Turning away, the two hoods headed for the
door and Abby sank against the tires.

"You okay?" Gary asked, wiping some blood
from his chin and attempting to smile.

"I . . . I guess. Oh, Gary." She ran to him
and threw her arms around his neck.

He wrapped his arms around her for a second and then let her go. "I thought I told you
to stay put."

"I was afraid . . . for you." She stepped back
and surveyed the damage to his handsome
face. "You look awful."

"Thanks a lot."

"You were lucky this time, Gary." Her blue
eyes were dark with concern as she pushed a
sweaty lock of his hair out of his eyes. She saw
him wince when she inadvertently touched a
cut over his eye. "What's going to happen
tomorrow?"

"I don't know, Abby. I just don't know."

She shook her head and stared up at him.
"Don't be a fool. You know that you can go
see J.R. and he'll help. It's your only chance.

Gary, it's only a loan, and when everything is done, you'll be able to pay him off and have a bankroll left over for the company. What's wrong with that?''

He walked away from her and started piling the tires back into a neat stack. "We've been over this before, Abby. You don't understand J.R. It will never be over and I'll be in his debt forever, believe me.''

"Okay, but forgive me if I fail to see your big alternative plan. You've got till tomorrow to come up with fifty thousand dollars, and as far as I can see, you've got about as much chance of doing that as digging for oil with a tooth-pick.''

Gary slumped against the wall and his eyes searched the ceiling. Everything Abby said was true—but that didn't make it right. If he went to his brother, J.R. would be in control of his life again. Once before, J.R. had almost destroyed him.

Jaw clenched tight, he straightened the tools and tried to come up with another solution. Unfortunately, there was none.

"Okay, Abby. You win. I'll call. I don't suppose you have the number?''

"Right here.'' She reached into her purse, extracted J.R.'s business card, and handed it to Gary.

He took it and turned it over. On the back, printed in J.R.'s bold writing, was the number and room of a local hotel. Gary's gut wrenched and his jaw ached from clenching it so tight. But he was out of options, and he had to try to make the best of a bad situation.

Walking over to Sid's phone, he dialed the number of J.R.'s hotel.

Two hours later Gary was standing in front of his brother feeling about two inches tall. He buried his balled fists deep in his pockets and waited for J.R. to get done with business. The sooner Gary could get out of the hotel room, the better for everyone.

Seated at the French provincial desk in his penthouse suite, J.R. carefully wrote out a check for fifty thousand dollars, made payable to Gary Ewing. Capping his pen and slipping it into his breast coat pocket, J.R. handed the check to his brother.

"There we go. No problem at all." J.R. chuckled.

Gary took the check but didn't bother looking at it. He nodded to J.R. and squeezed out a quiet, "Thanks."

"Happy to help you out—I mean, help out your friend." He paused to sip from his glass of bourbon. "I've been thinking, Gary. That fifty thousand'll buy you a mess of parts, didn't you say?"

Gary nodded, but didn't say a word. His nostrils flared and his blue eyes were trained on his brother.

"Well, what if you had a hundred thousand?"

Gary shrugged and walked to the door.

"What would you do with a hundred thousand dollars?" J.R. persisted.

"Make a bigger deal," Gary said, crossing his arms over his chest. What was J.R. getting at?

"You don't say. I bet you could lock up every

nut and bolt needed for the cars you sell."

"Yeah?"

"Give you a hell of an edge on your competition."

"I don't have a hundred thousand, though."

"If you did, you could undercut prices."

"So?"

"Have everybody eating out of your hands."

"I don't *have* a hundred thousand dollars," Gary repeated.

"And all for Sid Fairgate."

J.R. was baiting him and he knew it, but Gary kept up the charade. He had no choice. "For Sid. Yes."

J.R. slammed his boot to the ground. "No, it's not. It's for Gary Ewing! Maybe you came in for Sid, but since I brought up the hundred grand you haven't mentioned his name once."

Gary grinned coldly. "That's 'cause you've been doing all the talking, J.R."

"Admit it, Gary . . . all this is for you."

Gary leaned against the door and silently watched his brother, who was sitting on the edge of the desk.

"And there's not a damned thing wrong with that. It's what makes us Ewings strong."

"Rich, anyway."

"Same thing," J.R. said with a large grin.

Impatiently, Gary straightened and placed his hat on his head. "Are we through here, J.R., or what?"

"You've got your check, don't you?"

"Yeah."

Gary glanced down at the check and suddenly noticed that it wasn't signed. Looking up

at J.R., he felt all the muscles in his back grow
taut. ''You didn't sign it.''

J.R. looked at him innocently. ''No?''

Gary began to simmer. He knew his brother
was playing with him, and his patience for the
game was gone. ''Are you lending me the
money or not?''

''Oh, yes sir, I am, but I figure it entitles me
to make a little speech first.''

J.R. took back the check as if he were about
to sign it. Walking across the room, he looked
out the window for a second and then turned
to his brother. ''You're no more interested in
Sid Fairgate than I am.''

Gary bristled. ''Sid happens to be a good—''

''You're not talking Sid, Gary. You're talking
power. You're talking adrenalin and how it
surges through your veins when you get a
pocketful of something everybody else wants.
You're talking about *winning* for a change,
Gary. *Winning*, like a Ewing wins!'' Striding
back to Gary, J.R. tore up the check in front of
him and let the pieces flutter to the carpet.

Gary watched in stunned silence. It was over.
He'd have to tell Frank and Roy that he
didn't—*couldn't*—get the money. He'd have to
come clean with Val and Sid . . .

J.R. walked over to the desk and reached
behind the wastebasket. He pulled out a large
black attaché case and plunked it on the table
in front of Gary. ''Open it,'' he commanded.

Gary reached for the tabs and pulled them
away to spring open the top. The lid flew open.
Neat stacks of hundred dollar bills filled the
interior of the briefcase to the brim.

J.R. looked his brother straight in the eye.

Gary didn't flinch.

"This is real money. Take it. You see, doing business with your family doesn't have to be all bad."

Gary stared at the money in stunned disbelief. Simultaneously, he felt relief and caution. Relief won out. Carefully closing the briefcase, he slid it off the table. "Thank you."

J.R. clasped an arm around his brother's neck and walked with him to the door. "You let me know how you make out, now."

Gary nodded. "I will."

J.R. watched as Gary waited by the elevator, then came over to him as he was about to enter the slowly opening doors. Reaching into the elevator, J.R. placed his finger over the hold button and turned to his brother.

"One more thing, Gary."

Here it comes, Gary thought. "Yeah?"

"I've been thinking abut that engine of Sid's. Seems to me that something like that's got to be handled just right—with a proper combination of brains and guts and money. Otherwise, the chance of someone's lifetime might just slip right through his fingers."

"I'm sure you have . . . been thinking about it."

"Right." J.R. smiled and slapped him on the back. "You and I ought to make a point of talking about that sometime. Real soon."

Gary stared at his brother and then down at the attaché case. J.R. stepped back and released the elevator button and waved Gary through the open door.

"See you later, Gary. I'll be sure to kiss the folks back home for you."

The elevator doors slammed shut.

"You do that," Gary muttered.

Abby sat by the phone waiting for Gary's call. He had promised to report to her as soon as his meeting with J.R. was over. She was working on her third cup of coffee and slowly making herself a nervous wreck.

She had had enough experience in dealing with J.R. in the past few days to appreciate the difficulties that Gary would face. Now she could only hope that all her efforts would pay off.

"Five more minutes. That's all I can stand. If I don't hear from him in five minutes I'm going to the hotel myself," Abby told herself as she eyed the clock. "Damn it, Gary, call."

It would be just like J.R. to pull some stunt at the last minute and then take off for Dallas.

She stared at the phone and then plopped down in one of the kitchen chairs. "God, I can't stand this!"

Karen gathered her purse and shopping list and walked to the stairs. She'd told Sid about Jeff dropping the custody suit, but couldn't bring herself to tell him about the cryptic remarks that Jeff had made after his night with Abby. "The less said, the better," she told herself. "Karen, keep your nose in your own business!" But she couldn't shake the feeling that Jeff wasn't through fighting for Olivia and Brian.

"Diana?" she called up the stairs.

"Yeah?"

"I'm just going to the store for a few minutes. I won't be gone long. Will you stick around?"

"Sure."

Diana came out of her room and hung her head over the rail.

"Need anything?"

"Ten bucks?" she asked hopefully.

Karen laughed. "Don't we all. Look, I'll be right back."

"Okay, Mom. Michael and I are playing Monopoly."

"Great!"

"No hurry, Mom. Michael and I are having a good time."

Karen picked up her keys and walked out of the house feeling on top of the world.

Abby had waited five minutes, and five minutes beyond that, and five minutes longer still until she thought she would go stark raving mad. She couldn't sit around waiting another second. She grabbed her purse and keys and headed out the front door, intent on driving to J.R.'s hotel.

When she walked outside, she saw Karen getting into her car. Karen saw Abby's anxious face and made up her mind to straighten things out with her sister-in-law.

"Congratulations," she said, walking across the street. "I hear Jeff is dropping the custody suit."

"Yes, thank God." She had received a call

earlier from Jeff, who had told her of his new decision.

Karen decided to sink her teeth in a little. "Anything to win, right? No holds barred?"

"Save it, Karen! I didn't have to twist Jeff's arm. He knew what he was doing."

"It's too bad you don't," Karen murmured. If only Abby would quit scheming!

"No? He's gone, isn't he?" she said, smiling triumphantly.

"You've won this battle, but I'm afraid you've got a war on your hands," Karen said, thinking again about Jeff's parting remarks. "I'm afraid it's not over, Abby . . . it's only the beginning."

Karen turned and started to walk back toward her car. She really didn't know what Jeff had in mind, but she couldn't resist sinking the barb into Abby. After all the trouble she'd caused Sid and the Ewings, Abby had it coming. And the ominous tone of Jeff's voice had convinced her that there was, indeed, more to come.

"What are you talking about?" Abby shouted as Karen reached her car.

Karen didn't bother to answer. After all, it was Abby's problem, not hers.

"What are you talking about?"

Karen started the engine and began backing up.

"The beginning of what?" Abby yelled at her, but she didn't reply. Over the muffled roar of her engine, Karen could no longer hear her neighbor.

Abby stood in the middle of the street, absolutely bewildered. She'd won, hadn't she? Jeff was gone. He was going to drop the custody suit. So what in the world was Karen hinting about?

"Probably nothing," she told herself as she walked to her car, but she couldn't quite convince herself that Jeff wasn't ready for another battle. "Just let him try," she said, throwing open the door. "I'm ready for anything he's got planned!"